BEGUILED

THE FAIREST MAIDENS
TWO

Books by Jody Hedlund

Knights of Brethren Series
Enamored
Entwined
Ensnared
Enriched
Enflamed
Entrusted

The Fairest Maidens Series
Beholden
Beguiled
Besotted

The Lost Princesses Series
Always: Prequel Novella
Evermore
Foremost
Hereafter

Noble Knights Series
The Vow: Prequel Novella
An Uncertain Choice
A Daring Sacrifice
For Love & Honor
A Loyal Heart
A Worthy Rebel

Waters of Time Series
Come Back to Me
Never Leave Me
Stay With Me

The Colorado Cowboys
A Cowboy for Keeps
The Heart of a Cowboy

To Tame a Cowboy
Falling for the Cowgirl
The Last Chance Cowboy

The Bride Ships Series
A Reluctant Bride
The Runaway Bride
A Bride of Convenience
Almost a Bride

The Orphan Train Series
An Awakened Heart: A Novella
With You Always
Together Forever
Searching for You

The Beacons of Hope Series
Out of the Storm: A Novella
Love Unexpected
Hearts Made Whole
Undaunted Hope
Forever Safe
Never Forget

The Hearts of Faith Collection
The Preacher's Bride
The Doctor's Lady
Rebellious Heart

The Michigan Brides Collection
Unending Devotion
A Noble Groom
Captured by Love

Historical
Luther and Katharina
Newton & Polly

JODY HEDLUND

NORTHERN LIGHTS PRESS

MERCIA
OCEANUS
INGLEWOOD FOREST
HUNTWELL FORTRESS
BIRCHWOOD
BOARSHEAD HUNTING GROUNDS
GEMSTONE MOUNTAIN RANGE
RUBY MOUNTAIN
KENSINGTON
CAMBRIAN LOWLANDS
ROCKLAND
FOOTHILL PLAINS
GRAYSON
WARWICK
SICCUM DESERT
EAST SEA
GREAT ISLE

Chapter

1

Mikkel

Thick fog swirled around our boat like steam rising from a cauldron.

"We should return to camp." I glanced around, unable to see past the white mist that hedged us in on every side. For midmorning, the fog was unusual in the estuary. "Something in the air bodes of evil."

At the bow, Fowler tilted up his head and sniffed the air as if he were a hunting dog searching for prey. "Nay, the morn mist be hugging the shore longer this day. 'Tis naught more to it."

"Sir Gregor?" I paused in hefting up the hemp net, which was wriggling under the weight of the salmon, trout, and flounder left by the tide when the water had dashed back to the sea. "What say you? Shall we make this our last haul and return to camp?"

Gregor peered into the woven reed baskets surrounding him at the stern. Even with his left eye covered by a black patch, he saw more than most people with perfect vision. "Perchance. We do have over half our catch."

Fowler pulled at his end of the net, straining against the load. As a dwarf, his arms and legs were short, but they were also thick with bulging muscles. "The master'll string us up and pelt us with rotten fish carcasses if we be returning without full baskets."

The master would do no such thing. Blade might have a severe name and was spiteful toward his enemies. But in the two months I'd lived with his band on the Isle of Outcasts, he'd never been cruel to his own men.

At a splashing and plopping of water somewhere in the mist behind us, my spine stiffened. I peered around us, but there was nothing but fog. Even so, I sensed danger closing in. "What if the rumors about the Loch Ness monster awakening during the day are true?"

Fowler shook his head. "Nay. Couldn't be. She ever only hunts at night."

"But we cannot discount the recent sightings of her at dawn. And we cannot discount the possibility that all our fishing during the day might leave her with little to prey upon at night."

Before coming to the island, I'd assumed the giant man-eating sea monster was nothing more than a creature of myths. However, the outcasts swore Loch Ness lived in the deep waters surrounding the isle.

On several occasions in the moonlight, I'd sighted an eel-like head poking out of the water. Part of me wished to hunt down and kill the beast. But the perpetuation of the frightening tales of the Loch Ness monster kept the outside world from venturing to the island and spewing their hate at the outcasts.

Except for the Inquisitor . . .

I paused, straining to see and hear beyond the low cloud covering. Was the zealous witch hunter closing in on us?

Several feet away, a dark form took shape in the mist, then vanished. Someone—or something—was drawing nigh.

"Fie upon you, Mikkel," Fowler groused. "Stop your worrying and do your work. I may be an unusually strong man, but even I cannot be lifting this net on my own."

I wanted to command him to silence, but whoever was out there had probably already heard us and knew our location. Instead, as I resumed hauling in my end of the net, I met Gregor's gaze and attempted to communicate silently for him to be alert.

With oars lying idle in both hands, Gregor nodded and examined the mist too. His profile was normal, with smooth skin and perfect features. But as he shifted his head, the other side of his face, the one with the eye patch, came into view, revealing misshapen skin, puckered and splotchy from his temple down to his jaw and neck. The burn scars continued over most of the left half of his body, covering his arm and hand.

Since the May morn on the wharf when my father's weapons master had introduced me to Gregor, I'd been curious how my scribe had sustained such serious burns. But he hadn't offered an explanation, and I hadn't pried. It had been enough to know the Lagting had chosen Gregor for me because his appearance gave us the excuse we needed to take up residence on the Isle of Outcasts.

Set off the western coast of Norland, the island with its thick forests and large rock formations, had become a refuge for the outcasts of society, particularly those with physical differences and deformities such as Gregor's. In addition to being misfits, many were hardened criminals.

During the voyage from my home in Scania to the island, Gregor and I had discussed strategy and decided the only way the outcasts would allow someone like me, without limitations, onto the island was if Gregor posed as a noble lord and I accompanied him as his servant.

So far, our ruse had worked. While many questioned why Gregor needed to bring a manservant, no one realized I was Prince Mikkel of Scania, the firstborn son of King Christian of the Holberg lineage. I'd played my role well, treating Gregor as my lord, having to compensate at times for my scribe's difficulty in ordering me around.

Whenever Gregor protested, I assured him this was all part of my Testing, that the small deception was necessary in order to gain access to living amongst the outcasts. They accepted him as one of their own, and in doing so, tolerated my presence. At the very least, they'd ceased shunning me completely, as they'd done for weeks after we first arrived.

Gregor shifted on his bench, staring into the fog, rigid with readiness, obviously sensing the same peril I did.

"See you something, my lord?" I asked.

"Yes," he whispered tersely. "Someone is there."

Fowler stopped laboring. "If you sense danger, my lord, then we need be heading back."

I'd learned that Fowler and the others sought Gregor's approval because of his title. I found it both odd and enlightening to be disregarded as a servant when I was accustomed to people catering to my every word. I'd once believed my subjects deferred to me for my merit, but now I suspected it was largely because of my position as a prince.

The observation was one amongst many I'd made as I strove to fulfill the purpose of my Testing to *look on the heart.*

With a curt hand motion, Fowler indicated that we

release our catch of fish and head to shore. Carefully, I lowered the stone sinkers, trying to prevent them from splashing against the calm water. As we emptied the net, Gregor dipped the oars in deeply, letting the motion of the waves aid his effort.

Look on the heart. My thoughts flitted back to the day in the spring when my two brothers and I had received our commissioning for the Royal Testing that would determine which of us was worthy to become the next king of Scania. Birth order was no guarantee of kingship. Instead, a group of wise advisors called the Lagting sent each prince to a different place to prove himself by facing and enduring hardships for six months.

As an outsider trying to ingratiate myself among outcasts, my Testing had proven to be challenging, likely more so than Vilmar's. Sentenced to be a slave, all Vilmar had needed to do was show up at the Gemstone Mountains in Warwick and work. Excavating jewels would be difficult, and he'd face hunger and deprivations. But he was no doubt enjoying his friendships and charming his way out of any difficulties.

Vilmar had also probably charmed his scribe into writing pages upon pages of accolades to take back to the king and Lagting. Even without his scribe's glowing review of his Testing, the Lagting had always favored Vilmar, the outgoing and friendly prince. And 'twas no secret many of them wanted him to be the next king.

I drew my brows together in a scowl. My brother was an honest man full of integrity. I had no doubt he'd make an excellent king if God willed it, but I wasn't ready to concede now any more than I'd ever been. It took much more to lead a nation than popularity and friendliness.

As I dragged the net back inside the boat and dropped

it into the hull, I reached for the other pair of oars. Fowler hopped up onto the front bench, standing at the ready, his hunting knife drawn.

Another boat containing half a dozen men emerged from the mist and scraped our hull. With tightening muscles, I dropped the oars and lunged for my spear, but with the net thrown in haphazardly, my fingers fumbled to find the handle. Shouts erupted around us, and new footfalls thumped into our boat, rocking it and weighing it down.

Abandoning my efforts at wielding my spear, I jumped to my feet with my knife in hand. Though I was most proficient with a spear, I was skilled with any weapon. My father's weapons master had made sure of that. Before my attacker could swing, I ducked, pivoted, and grabbed him in a headlock, pressing my blade against his chest.

Ahead, Fowler exchanged sword blows with another intruder. And behind me Gregor was doing the same. A quick look told me all I needed to know. Irontooth's band was assailing us.

Of all the threats facing us this morn, I'd neglected to consider our rivals on the island. In truth, I had no issue with the other group of outcasts. I'd never met them, had only seen the several Blade had recently captured and enslaved. From what I could tell, they were no different or worse in their physical limitations than anyone in our group. And yet, the bands had been warring with each other for years.

Now with one of Irontooth's outcasts within my grip and arms pinned at his back, I was loathe to hurt the poor soul. If not for fate, he could have been my companion during my Testing instead of Fowler. Gregor and I had just happened to land on the area of the island closest to

Blade's camp and had been intercepted by his men instead of Irontooth's.

The clang of metal and the grunts of fighting rose into the fog. I needed to put an end to the skirmish to prevent anyone from sustaining serious injury.

"Hold your weapons!" I repositioned my blade against my captive's neck, which was covered with a strange black material. "And your man will remain safe."

"Man?" said a decidedly feminine voice from the person I was holding.

I dropped my gaze to find a pair of beguiling green eyes peering at me. Even though the black silky material rose above my captive's nose, leaving the top quarter of the face visible, I was left with no doubt that this was a woman—a very comely woman.

"Unhand me." She spoke smoothly, though her voice was somewhat muffled behind the veil. "As you can see, I am no man."

Yes, I could see that. This was no mere peasant or tradesman's daughter. Something in her tone and the way she held herself told me she was a woman of some bearing, perhaps of noble birth.

I let my knife fall away. I would have released a poor woman too. I wasn't predisposed to the rich. Was I?

Before I could figure out my next step, the woman twisted out of my grasp and elbowed me with a force that left me gasping for breath. Then before I knew what she was doing, she bent, grasped me from behind, and flipped me over her back. I landed in the hull with a crack that knocked any remaining air from my lungs.

An instant later, she was standing upon my arms, this time with her knife pressed against my neck. "Hold your weapons." Her bright eyes captured mine as she mocked me with the words I'd spoken moments earlier. "And your man will remain safe."

I attempted to move my hands to protect myself, but the heels of her boots ground into my wrists, and excruciating pain shot up my arm.

From the quiet at the back of the boat, I could tell Gregor had stopped fighting his opponent. But ahead, Fowler continued to battle a man twice his size with an abnormally big head and enormous ears.

Even though Fowler fought valiantly, he lurched about and bumped into the side of the boat. The rocking motion threw him off balance, and he started to fall overboard. His opponent grabbed him, placing a swift blow across his head and knocking him out.

The woman on top of me didn't let up on the pressure on my wrists, and I gritted my teeth to keep from shouting at her.

As though recognizing my self-control, her eyes flashed with more mocking humor. "See that you and your manservant cooperate." She nodded toward Gregor. "Or you will both be rendered unconscious too."

My servant? How did this woman know Gregor was my servant and not my master?

She gave a disdainful bow. "My lord, you do not belong on this island. And Irontooth aims to find out who you are and why you are here."

Chapter 2

Pearl

My prisoner was handsome. I don't know why that fact stood out to me, but it did nonetheless. Strands of his shoulder-length fair hair were plaited into small braids on one side of his face. The scruffy layer of stubble on his jaw and chin was slightly darker in coloring, making the blue of his eyes all the brighter and more alluring. The rest of his features—his nose, mouth, cheekbones—were flawless, almost regal.

While spying, Toad had heard the eye-patch man calling his companion Mikkel and ordering him around. In return, Mikkel had addressed the eye-patch man as Sir Gregor. Toad hadn't been exaggerating when he said Mikkel didn't belong on the island and that he carried himself with the bearing of a lord.

One well-placed word on my part had confirmed the truth: Mikkel was not a servant.

He bucked against me so sharply and suddenly my hold upon his hands wavered. He took advantage of my inattention by rolling away from my boots and blade. An instant later he was on his feet, a spear in his hand aimed at me.

Not only was he noble and handsome, but he was well trained.

Fortunately, I was also well trained after living on the island for the past year and spending every spare moment learning all I could about weaponry and fighting. Before he could make another move, I had my bow up and an arrow pointed at him.

"Go ahead and throw your spear . . . if you wish to die today."

With a sweeping glance, he took in the boat behind me with three of my companions inside, all wielding weapons at the ready. Then his gaze rested upon me. Wearing a man's tunic, breeches, and boots, I made a dismal picture, though his narrowed eyes revealed naught, not even the repugnance I was certain he must be feeling at seeing a woman attired as a man. He was surely also wondering what deformity I was covering with my veil.

Irontooth and Felicity were the only two who knew the truth about my veil and why I was hiding behind it. Once I'd revealed my identity to them, they'd agreed I would be safer if no one else knew. Never in all the months since then had I felt the urge to show myself. Until this moment . . .

For a reason I couldn't explain, I wished I could give this fine-looking stranger a glimpse of my face and earn his appreciation, not his disdain.

Slowly, he lowered his spear. "I have no wish to meet my Maker this day . . . my lady." His blue eyes challenged me to deny his use of the title. In some ways he was right. I was nobility. But I was also so much more. Or was I? When I ran away from Warwick last summer, I left behind my title, power, and rights. And when my mother had proclaimed the news of the hunting accident and my death, perhaps Princess Pearl truly died after all.

Perhaps Veil was all who remained.

"Want us to tie 'em up, Veil?" Toad asked from where he stood with his knife pressed against Gregor.

"Yes. Start with Mikkel and Gregor. We shall bind Fowler last." I didn't take my attention from Mikkel and took pleasure when his eyes widened again at the use of their given names.

"I regret that you know more about us than we do about you, my lady." He didn't resist as Humphrey disarmed him and jerked his hands behind his back.

"'Tis not enough for Irontooth. In fact, 'twill not be enough until he has wrung the truth from you. One way or another."

"I shall be more than willing to speak with Irontooth." Mikkel showed confidence and none of the fear I'd wanted to instill. "I've been hoping to have an audience with him. And now, I shall have my chance."

Several of our band had been captured last week by Blade's outcasts, and Irontooth had decided to abduct these newest recruits in retaliation. Of course, I'd offered to lead the expedition, since I needed all the practice in kidnapping I could get. Then when I returned to the palace in Kensington, I'd be able to spirit Ruby away without the queen's knowledge.

Just the merest thought of my younger sister twisted a knot inside, the one that had formed the day I'd been forced to leave her behind.

The day the queen had set out to murder me.

As it was, I hadn't known anything until it was too late, and I had barely escaped with my life.

During my long days of hiding and running, I'd sobbed many silent tears for the sweet child who would be devastated when she received the news of my death. I'd contemplated sending her a note and letting her know I was alive.

However, every time I started to pen a letter, I stopped. At twelve, Ruby was still too young to keep a secret from the queen, and communication would put us both in more peril.

I'd only been able to pray for her these long months we'd been apart, that God would give her strength in her grief. At least Ruby had her friendship with the nuns who lived in the abbey connected with Kensington Cathedral. Since Father's death, she'd requested visits from them almost daily, beseeching them for prayer and comfort. Now in my absence, I was trusting the dear women to do whatever they could to take care of my sister.

And I lived with the hope that soon—very soon—I'd be able to escape with Ruby from Warwick to a new place where we could start over and never again have to worry about the manipulations of our mother.

A shiver raced up my backbone, one filled with the chill of not only all I'd left behind in my old life but also of approaching danger. I peered into the mist, searching for shadows and listening for the sounds of a vessel. Though I heard nothing, the trepidation remained.

"Time to go," I said quietly.

Toad and Humphrey finished binding the prisoners, and then after dividing them between the two boats, we hunkered down and rowed around the island. The fog was no barrier to us, since we were accustomed to maneuvering in all conditions. Our prisoners remained silent and cooperative, clearly sensing we were not the only enemies they must worry about.

By the time we reached the far western shore, an ocean breeze rolling in with the waves pushed against the fog, lifting it and leaving a gentle rain in its place. We rowed into one of the narrow inlets and stowed the boats under the thick evergreen branches that bowed against the water.

Fowler had long since roused and had the sense not to cause any trouble. We chained all three prisoners together in a line and marched up the rocky path toward the caves we called home. I fell into step beside Mikkel, the clinking of the prisoners' chains nearly drowned out by the rushing of the river in the gorge below.

The more information I could get from him before arriving at camp, the better. Somehow I needed to impress Irontooth and prove I was ready to launch my rescue of Ruby.

"From whence do you come?" I asked.

He cast me a glance, one filled with curiosity. "I shall tell you if you're willing to reveal the same about yourself."

"Very well. I hail from Warwick." I'd perfected the tale of my being an outcast months ago and could so easily speak the lies interwoven with the truth that I could hardly distinguish one from the other anymore. "My family lives in Kensington."

"I am from Scania. My family lives in Bergen during the winter and Trommen for the summer months."

Scania was at least one week away, if not two, by boat. Why was a nobleman from a foreign country on the Isle of Outcasts? "You are far from home."

"Yes, I miss my homeland." A wistful note in his voice revealed his sincerity. "Although, I admit to taking a liking to Norland. She's a beautiful country and reminds me of Scania."

As the northernmost country of the Great Isle, Norland had a colder climate and more mountainous terrain than either Mercia or Warwick. And Norland was home to many small islands off her coast, most uninhabitable.

Though low clouds still hung over our island, the rugged hills partially covered in thick pine and fir rose around us. The path beneath our boots was rock and dirt made smooth from the many feet traversing it over the years. But on either side, the crags were jagged and hostile.

I'd hiked the width of the island once, and crossing the rocky terrain had taken me the better part of a day. The length was at least double the width, which provided plenty of space for the two groups of warring outcasts to remain far away from each other. Blade's band took the southern part of the island, and our band lived on the northern end.

"You speak the language of the Great Isle well," I said. Only men and women of high birth were versed in foreign languages, the result of years of tutoring. I knew because it was true of myself.

"My mother is from the Great Isle." He hesitated, as if he was giving too much about himself away. "While I was growing up, she spoke little else but her native language around me."

I had not heard of nobility marrying outside their country of birth. Royalty often did so for political alliances, but what reason did his mother have to marry a nobleman from Scania? "What brings you to Norland and this isle?"

He shot a glance toward his servant, who walked several paces ahead. "Gregor."

After living amongst the outcasts of society for the past year, I no longer noticed the differences in their appearances. But now, I studied Gregor, taking in the burns covering half his body. The scarred man spoke little but seemed to see and hear everything. Perhaps, like many of the other outcasts, he'd gained heightened sensory awareness to make up for his deficiencies.

"You don't strike me as the type of man willing to make so great a sacrifice for someone so insignificant to you."

"And who says Gregor is insignificant?"

"You need not say it. 'Tis clear enough without words."

Mikkel's brows furrowed into thunderheads, and his heavy steps drew to a halt, jerking both Gregor and Fowler to a stop as well. Several of the men in the lead grumbled and cajoled Fowler, who proceeded to mock them in return, earning a slap in the face.

At the sight of Fowler's trouble, Mikkel started up again, but this time he slowed his steps. I hoped he was rethinking his answer and would elaborate more, but instead he changed the subject. "Your turn, my lady. What brings you to Norland and this isle?"

"Is it not obvious?" I resituated my veil.

"Did your family scorn you for—for your blemishes?" He slanted a look toward the veil, then focused on the steeply rising trail ahead, but not before I saw pity in his eyes.

Most of the outcasts believed I concealed deformities of one kind or another behind my veil. And so far, none of their assumptions had bothered me. But with Mikkel's curiosity—and pity—I couldn't keep my embarrassment at bay. I didn't want him thinking I was hideous.

As before, I had the urge to lift the silk and show him the truth, that I had skin as perfect and smooth as the pearl after which I was named. My flawless features, womanly figure, and long ebony hair had drawn the admiration of many. Brave knights had written poems about me. Wealthy lords had pledged me their fealty. Foreign diplomats had offered marriage proposals on behalf of their princes and kings.

"I am truly sorry." He apparently took my silence as affirmation. "Families ought to be a place of unconditional acceptance for who we are and encourage us in the potential for what we can yet become."

"Spoken wisely, my lord." I couldn't keep from studying this man. From all appearances, he wasn't much older than my nineteen years. Probably twenty-two or twenty-three years of age. "If you have found such acceptance and encouragement from your family, then you are indeed blessed."

He plodded uphill, growing silent once more, his expression unreadable.

I would likely get no more information from him than he would from me. Alas, Irontooth would find ways to extract what he wanted to know. And once he had, he'd assign Mikkel as a slave to one of the men. I'd speak little to the nobleman in the days to come. Soon the two feuding leaders would arrange an exchange of prisoners. Mikkel, Gregor, and Fowler would return to the southern part of the island, and I'd never cross paths with them again, especially once I left.

With the arrival of Midsummer's Eve last week, summer was passing too quickly. While the others in camp had danced and feasted to celebrate, I'd hiked to the top of one of my favorite arches and spent the eve in somber quietude. The solstice in my country had always been one of terror—the eve when the fairest maiden in the land was sacrificed to Grendel.

Like most maidens in Warwick, I'd lived with the worry that one day I might be considered the fairest maiden and given to Grendel to appease his rage. I'd feared my mother would do nothing to prevent it, might even be glad for it.

I'd never understood why my mother resented me. Of course, servants had whispered that she disliked me because I rivaled her beauty. Others said she was jealous because the king spent more time with his children than with his wife.

Father had indeed spent much time with us. I had many fond memories of my childhood with him. He'd loved to hunt, and when I'd grown old enough, he'd taken me with him on nearly every hunting expedition.

It wasn't until I was older I'd understood that in marrying Queen Margery, he'd gained the title of king but had few responsibilities and almost no authority. Fortunately, he'd had a pleasant temperament and easily deferred the decision making to the queen.

He'd disagreed with her over one issue—the yearly sacrifice to Grendel. He'd pleaded with her on more than one occasion to allow him to attempt to kill the beast, but she always refused, fearing too much for his life.

Of course, I'd been torn over the matter. On the one hand, I'd wanted my father to put an end to the custom as the dreaded Choosing Ball loomed ever nearer for me. On the other hand, I'd agreed with the queen that I didn't want him to die fighting Grendel.

When I'd voiced my fears to Father, he'd ruffled my hair and told me not to worry, that he'd always be there to make sure I was safe. If only that had been true . . .

And if only Mother hadn't seen me as a threat. Although my younger brother, Ethelbard, was first in line to inherit the throne, the queen feared I'd try to usurp her. The truth was, I had no aspirations to rule Warwick and had never even hinted at trying to take the throne from my mother or Ethelbard.

Yes, I'd heard the rumors amongst courtiers that I'd make a better ruler than the queen and Ethelbard combined. Nevertheless, I'd never taken such talk seriously. I attributed the discontentment to the growing poverty in Warwick, especially as the nation's main industry, the gem mines, had produced fewer of the emeralds, rubies, sapphires, and diamonds that had once been excavated in abundance.

Whatever the case, my mother had never accepted or encouraged me. Not in the least. And in those last few years after Father's heart attack, our relationship had grown more strained. Even so, I hadn't expected her to plot my death . . .

A sharp pain flared to life inside. My mother, my own flesh and blood, had tried to have me murdered. If she hated me so much, why hadn't she simply chosen me to be the offering to Grendel? After all, the Choosing Ball had been less than a month away. She could have waited for Grendel to kill me and saved herself from having blood on her hands.

A shrill bird call told me the lookout had spotted our return and alerted Irontooth and the others. At the crest of the hill, our path leveled off and narrowed. The heavy pine boughs overhead shadowed us, making the day appear gloomier than it was.

"This warring between the two bands of outcasts is unnecessary." Mikkel searched the treetops and paused at each of our lookouts, finding them too easily, though they were well hidden.

The longer I was with our prisoner, the more I was convinced he was no ordinary nobleman. Though I'd distracted him to my advantage in the boat when I'd overtaken him, he was undeniably a skilled warrior. In addition, everything about him from the way he spoke to his bearing indicated he had a purpose for being on the island. And it had nothing to do with his servant. Irontooth was justified in his desire to capture and question this man.

Was he a spy? Perhaps for the Inquisitor?

I nearly stumbled at the thought and caught myself before anyone noticed. Surely he couldn't be a spy, not after living on the island for two months. Blade would have figured out the duplicity by now and killed him.

"I don't understand why both groups don't join forces," he continued. "If we work together, we'll be stronger and better equipped for fighting the real adversaries."

I released a scoffing laugh. "Blade and Irontooth are

sworn enemies. They have despised each other for as long as they both have lived."

"What is the cause of such animosity?"

"It is of no consequence." In truth, I didn't know what had turned them against each other. The one time I'd dared to ask Irontooth, he'd yelled at me for five full minutes and then stormed out of the cave. I hadn't asked again since.

"It *is* of consequence." The chains around Mikkel's hands and ankles clinked together as he walked ahead of me now. "One should bridge the rifts if at all possible."

"Perhaps that is true in your world, but not in mine." After the malevolence my mother had heaped upon me, I had no wish to bridge our rift. In fact, I'd rejoice if I never had to see her again.

Before Mikkel could speak further, shouting and jeers clamored from the path ahead. The misfits who made their home amongst the caves had come out, brandishing their weapons, ready to give the newcomers their usual greeting.

Fowler, at the front of the line of prisoners, came to an abrupt halt. Gregor's face remained expressionless, but Mikkel's features hardened, and he stiffened his shoulders, evidently surmising the welcome would be anything but pleasant.

Chapter 3

MIKKEL

I braced myself for the gauntlet. Outcasts both short and tall lined the trail, wielding an odd assortment of weapons from maces to red-hot irons to knives. Their faces contorted as they yelled out their fury.

If I'd been under any illusion that my capture would be easy, it had vanished. This was no game. It was, in fact, a deadly ritual.

I'd never run through a gauntlet before, but I'd heard about the barbaric practice in my studies. Sometimes prisoners didn't make it through the blows alive. Most often, they became maimed and scarred for life.

Was that what this was about? Did these outcasts enjoy hurting people the way they themselves had been hurt? Did they hope to make others suffer? Or did they want to disfigure those like me who weren't deformed enough?

Now wasn't the time to analyze their motives. I needed to devise a plan to protect not only myself but also Gregor and Fowler.

As one of our captors began to free us from our chains, I stepped closer to my scribe. "If you go directly behind me, I shall be able to shield you from most of the blows."

"No." Gregor eyed the menagerie of weapons ahead the same way I had. "I'll go before you and take the blows first. You stay at my rear."

I shook my head, refusing to let this man suffer any more than he already had. "I insist."

"And I insist as well."

The woman with the veil stepped between us. "As touching as your display for each other is," she whispered, irritation flashing in her eyes, "I suggest you each attempt to take a weapon from someone at the beginning of the line and fight your way through."

"Will they allow it?" I asked.

"They will not stop you." She spun and strode toward the gauntlet.

My fascination with this strangely engaging woman grew with every passing moment. As she took her place at the front of the line, she unsheathed a knife. In the same instant, her attention dropped to her belt riding low on her hip and the sword still within its scabbard.

Was she sending me a message that she wouldn't prevent me from taking her sword? But what about Gregor? And Fowler? What weapons would aid them during their walk of death?

As if hearing my silent questions, the veiled woman glanced to the heavyset man across from her, to his leather boot. The upper edge of a knife handle poked out the top. Her gaze shifted to the man next to him and the long metal pipe he was twirling around.

Why was this woman giving us these tips on how to

survive the gauntlet? What did she have to gain?

A shout from behind us was followed by a shove. We were free of our chains and had to start running. I didn't wait for Fowler or Gregor. I charged forward without them. The sneering and scorning increased, drowning out my thudding heart along with Gregor's plea for me to stop.

As my feet picked up speed, I veered toward my first target—the sword. The woman with the veil made a move—albeit a weak one—to slash my arm, but I freed her sword and parried a blow from the person beside her. After doing so, I spun and tossed the weapon to Gregor. Then, I lunged and grabbed the knife from the boot. I jumped to avoid an axe blade swinging at my legs, but I couldn't dodge the hot iron hitting my upper arm, searing through my shirt and scorching my flesh.

I wanted to roar out my pain but held myself back. That would only feed the frenzy for more destruction. Instead, I swiped a metal cylinder in midair and used it to block a sword coming at me from the left.

Before moving farther into the fray, I passed the knife to Fowler. In that same instant, a mace swung at my head. Thankfully, Gregor deflected the blow with the sword.

He would have slipped past me to lead the charge, but I regained my balance and lurched ahead, swinging the lead pipe back and forth like a scythe, clearing the way and beating down most of the weapons aimed at me.

As the end drew nearer, my hand grew slick with blood, and my grip began to weaken. The blood along with the pain in my arm told me I was injured, but I pushed onward for what seemed an eternity until I stumbled out of the gauntlet.

I wanted to collapse in relief for having survived, but I

pivoted toward the last few men and engaged them again, distracting them while Gregor and Fowler both staggered past the onslaught and dropped to the ground.

The shouting continued for several more seconds before it tapered to silence. It took me a moment to realize the outcasts were staring at a man who had emerged from the path ahead. He wore a cloak made of fine silver threads that matched his silver hair and long beard. His face was scarred with white slashes across his cheek, forehead, chin, and even one through his lips, revealing glinting silver teeth beneath.

Irontooth. The leader of this rough group. He was flanked on one side by an abnormally burly man who seemed to be covered in hair over every inch of his body. On the other side stood a woman with pale lips and the purest, whitest hair I'd ever seen.

The silver-haired man strolled forward, his attention flicking from Fowler and Gregor back to me, where it held. His eyes were dark, piercing deeply, seeing past my exterior to all my secrets. He couldn't really read my mind. Still, I lowered myself to one knee and bowed my head, more to hide my thoughts than to show deference.

As his footsteps crunched nearer, I kept my head down until I found myself staring at a pair of iron-toed boots. I tensed with the uncertainty of what this leader would do.

The wind clattered the branches overhead, shaking moisture down upon my back. Or maybe it was more blood. The slice in my arm burned, and blood continued to trickle down to my hand, dripping from my fingertips to the rocky path.

"You and your man there." Irontooth's voice was steely. "Who sent you to our island?"

"No one. We've come of our own volition."

His hand connected with my cheek in a blow that would have sent me to the ground had I not been a strong man. Pain ricocheted through my face and into my head, but I held my body in place.

"You're lying." His tone grew sharper. "Are you the Inquisitor's spy?"

I raised my head so he could see the truth of my answer. "No. If you would allow me, I shall help rally your forces and lead a battle against the Inquisitor the next time he attempts to land on the island."

The citizens in Fife, across the Channel from the island, didn't like having the misfits living so close. Upon receiving their complaints, the Inquisitor had settled in Fife and made it his mission to eliminate the outcasts.

I wanted to suggest Irontooth join forces with Blade's army in battling the Inquisitor, but the veiled woman's warning about the animosity between the leaders stopped the words before I incurred more of Irontooth's wrath.

He narrowed his eyes upon me, clearly not trusting me even with my offer. "If not the Inquisitor, then who has dispatched you?"

"I'm here on behalf of Gregor." I nodded toward where my scribe and Fowler had collapsed, noting the blood and bruises on their faces. Hopefully, they'd fared no worse than I had with nothing but a few surface wounds.

Irontooth didn't take his attention from me. "Veil insists the manservant is here for you and not the other way."

The veiled woman was perceptive, and I couldn't deny the charge. Yet how else could I explain our presence on the island? "I brought him here for his own protection." It was the best excuse I could think of under duress.

But it apparently wasn't enough for Irontooth. His fist connected with my other cheek, this blow harder than the last. Blackness threatened to overtake me, and I fought against it, especially when I realized Gregor now stood over me, his sword clashing with Irontooth's.

Shouting erupted around us as several men worked to disarm and restrain Gregor. I struggled to my feet. At the sight of a blade pressed against Gregor's throat, I started to swing my weapon, only to find my arms wrenched behind my back.

The outcasts thrust me back to my knees in front of Irontooth.

Silence descended over the gathering again, and my heart thudded with a new fear, one I hadn't experienced since starting my Testing—the fear that we were in very real danger of losing our lives.

"I say throw them into the sea and feed them to Loch Ness," shouted a man from behind. Some chorused their agreement while others offered other suggestions.

Irontooth prodded me with the toe of his boot. "Tell me the truth, or I'll do as they say."

I bowed my head. I'd kept my identity as a prince of Scania hidden thus far. Once these outcasts realized I was a prince, they would most certainly expel me from the island, and I would have to forfeit my Testing. If they didn't kill me first.

"Why are you here?"

"Please believe me when I say I am no foe." I had to try one more time to broker for our lives. However, if I could not save us with my own ingenuity, then I would willingly give up the kingship, for I wouldn't be worthy of such a role. "I vow that I am your humble servant. I pledge to do your bidding so long as it remains in accordance with God's laws."

Once more the outcasts grew silent and waited for their leader's pronouncement. The damp air crackled around me with their anticipation.

I could feel Irontooth's sharp gaze upon my bent head, and I prayed he would accept my offer.

"Nay," he finally said.

As the cheers rose around us, my shoulders drooped with defeat.

"Feed them to the sea serpent!"

"Give me two weeks!" The veiled woman's voice rose above the others. "And I shall discover his true purpose for being here."

Calls of disdain and opposition followed the remark.

"If I do not succeed," she called louder, "then I shall help you turn them into fodder for Loch Ness."

How had I survived for two months in Blade's camp without rousing suspicion, and I'd been present in this camp for two minutes and they already wanted to kill me? I suspected this noblewoman was to blame. She'd recognized my status when no one else had. She'd pointed out my duplicity to Irontooth, who now feared my motives for being here.

Why, then, was she attempting to save me? Perhaps she'd thought to earn Irontooth's favor by bringing me to him but hadn't expected her master to so quickly sentence me to death. Whatever the case, I was at her mercy and prayed Irontooth would accept her offer.

"One week," Irontooth said. "You have one week to wrest the truth from them. If not, then we'll deliver them to Loch Ness."

I lifted my head and found Irontooth studying Veil,

who stood a few feet away. She met his hard gaze without flinching, her shoulders straight, her head angled up as though she was accustomed to giving orders. Would she protest her master's decision?

She hesitated for another heartbeat before bowing her head in submission.

The moment she was no longer looking at Irontooth, his stare softened, almost turned sad. And I knew without a doubt, he'd do anything for her. If I could win Veil's favor, I would win his.

Chapter 4

Pearl

"Chain them to the walls," *I commanded,* as I hopped down from the bottom rung of the ladder into the cave. Toad and Humphrey and several others pushed the prisoners deeper into the dank cavern we called our dungeon.

Guilt needled me. I'd almost cost these men their lives. I should have known Irontooth wouldn't be satisfied with anything less than the truth from Mikkel. But perhaps his secrets were too deep to unburden, especially so publicly. Mine were.

When I'd asked for two weeks, I'd known Irontooth would only give me one, and now I prayed that would be sufficient for discovering the real reason Mikkel was on the island.

I held my torch up, giving light to the dark cave with its low ceilings, smooth walls, and the dry pine boughs spread across the floor. It wasn't the cleanest spot in camp, but it wasn't as foul as the dungeons under the palace in Kensington.

Humphrey forced Mikkel to the floor and wrapped a manacle around his ankle.

"Bind Mikkel's hands and his feet."

Humphrey paused. I knew what he was thinking, that the prisoner would be helpless without his hands. But that was precisely what I wished for—for Mikkel to rely upon me for everything.

I stood back and watched as the men finished chaining the prisoners. Fowler complained the entire time, and Gregor didn't make a sound. Although Mikkel didn't speak either, his eyes communicated much more than words, mainly that he was in pain from the injuries he'd received during his run through the gauntlet.

From what I could tell, he'd sustained a gash near his jaw, along with burns and knife cuts on his arms. In taking the lead, he'd suffered the brunt of the brutality. He'd surprised me by refusing to allow his servant to protect him. Even more, he'd surprised me by taking the least effective weapon while giving Gregor and Fowler the means to defend themselves more sufficiently.

My astonishment had changed to admiration as Mikkel had advanced through the gauntlet so fearlessly, paving the way for Gregor and Fowler. He was clearly a good man who cared about his servant more than he did himself, perhaps proving my earlier statement wrong that Gregor was insignificant to him.

I was as curious as Irontooth to know who Mikkel really was and why he was here. Could I elicit the truth from him, or would he come up with a plausible excuse?

Humphrey stepped away from Mikkel, leaving both

arms and legs manacled. In so vulnerable a position, the nobleman was without the ability to stop me from doing anything I wished to him.

At the prospect, something strange fluttered in my stomach. He was handsome, one of the handsomest men I'd met. If only I didn't have to hide my face. Then I could use my beauty to win him over. I'd grown up watching my mother use her beauty to beguile people into doing her bidding, particularly my father. All she'd needed to do was peer at him with her mesmerizing eyes, curve her pretty lips, and whisper in his ear, and he became clay in her hands.

Over recent years, I'd realized my beauty was beguiling too, that it held some kind of power over men, almost as though it could cast a spell over them. When I'd first realized I wielded such influence, I was amused. But as time had passed, I grew frustrated that men saw only my outward appearance and paid little heed to anything else.

Dare I use my beguiling beauty to weave a spell over Mikkel and make him like clay in my hands? As appealing as the idea was, I cast it aside. I'd come to like the respect I earned from the outcasts for my actions and not for what I looked like. And I didn't want that to change.

I would have to win Mikkel's trust with other methods. I'd start by doctoring his wounds. Certainly the tender care would soften him. And I would befriend him so he'd think of me as an ally rather than an enemy.

After making sure the prisoners were well contained and guarded, I climbed out of the cavern into the rain that fell steadily and cast a chill over our camp. The low clouds and fog had returned, settling in amongst the rocky outcroppings and obscuring the half dozen cave entrances that made up the bulk of our dwellings. At the center of the camp, a large covering made of hides had been secured to four tall posts and provided a shelter during both rain and snow. A center hole in the hides allowed smoke from the fire pit to escape.

Felicity stood at the fire in front of a pot hanging from a tripod. The waft of fish told me she was cooking fish chowder, one of our usual fares. Next to her, Irontooth sipped from his large pewter stein covered in intricate raised engravings of knights doing battle. The lid was in the shape of a knight's helmet with fancy plumage rising and serving as the thumb lift. Irontooth didn't say so, but others speculated the stein had been a gift for his service and bravery from Norland's old king.

"Veil," he called as I attempted to sneak past. "I need to speak with you."

His tone was severe, and the others who'd been loitering under the shelter dispersed. I didn't blame them. Irontooth wasn't an easy master to please and even more difficult when he was irritated.

I wanted to call out that I'd meet with him later, but I suppressed my natural inclination to order people around as I always had in the days when I'd been a princess and forced myself to approach him.

Felicity remained at the pot, her expression serene. At my approach, her pale lips curved into a warm smile and her colorless eyes met mine, assuring me I had nothing to worry about.

I nodded in return, thankful for this friend. At least

a decade my senior, she'd taken me under her charge from the day I arrived and taught me how to survive in this rough wilderness. After I'd revealed to her my true identity as Princess Pearl of Warwick, Queen Margery's oldest child, she'd hadn't treated me differently. My royalty hadn't impressed her the way it did most people. At first I hadn't been sure I liked that. But now, after the many passing months, I realized her acceptance of all people regardless of station or stature was something I'd do well to emulate.

"What else did you learn of the prisoners?" Irontooth wiped foam from his mustache.

I relayed to him a summary of the few details I'd gleaned from Mikkel during our walk from the boat to camp. But it was a paltry amount, and I wasn't surprised when Irontooth guffawed. "You'd better get him to reveal more than that, or I will kill him."

"Have no fear. I shall succeed." I'd perfected the appearance of confidence over the years. "If you had watched him run the gauntlet, you would like him."

"Perhaps he should run it again, since all I'm hearing is how good he was."

"Perhaps he should. But first he needs his wounds cleaned, or you will indeed kill him from neglect."

"That's one way to do away with him."

"He deserves the benefit of the doubt until he proves otherwise."

"Until he betrays us all to the Inquisitor."

"You gave me a chance to prove myself," I said more gently and with a note of teasing. "And now you cannot imagine the camp without me in it."

Irontooth mumbled under his breath, then took a swig from his stein. Even with his severity, he was a caring man at heart.

"Perhaps he will be an asset," I added.

"Or he could be the ruin of us all." Irontooth's brow furrowed as he glanced in the direction of the dungeon. Older than my father by many years, Irontooth had become a father figure to me nonetheless.

"We are strong and capable of defending ourselves against one man."

"But he isn't like us."

I wanted to remind Irontooth I wasn't like the outcasts either. But the truth was, I no longer saw the differences. I only saw the ways we were all alike.

"Do whatever you need to in order to get the truth from him. And if you can't stomach torture, I'll send Tommy down to do it."

I followed Irontooth's gaze to the dungeon entrance, where Tommy stood guard. With the unnatural growth of thick hair covering his body, he almost resembled a bear. At times he acted like one. One of the biggest and most muscular men on the island, he was a ferocious fighter, sometimes too much so for my sensitive heart. "You gave me a week. I shall use my methods and shall not tolerate any interference."

"Take care." Irontooth lowered his voice. "He might be a spy for the queen."

I nodded. We'd discussed the possibility that the queen might know I was still alive. After all, when the huntsmen had returned without my body, the queen would have questioned them further. And what if she'd tortured and extracted information from the huntsman who'd set me free?

I needed no further urging from Irontooth to be careful. I had enemies on all sides, and I couldn't forget that. However, Mikkel was chained hand and foot to the dungeon wall. What harm could come of wresting more information from him this week by befriending and softening him so he would tell me all his secrets?

With a final word of assurance to Irontooth, I sped away and gathered medicinal supplies to tend to the prisoners' wounds. A short while later, Tommy opened the door and lowered the ladder. As I climbed down with my torch in hand and supplies in a bag over my shoulder, I could feel the prisoners watching me warily.

I hopped down, walked to the center, and then studied each of them, trying to decide if Fowler and Gregor had wounds that needed tending too. From what I could tell, they were nicked and bruised but would easily heal. Still, I crossed toward them.

"If you must inflict more pain," Mikkel said, "please spare them and abuse me instead."

I halted.

"I beg of you." His voice was strained. From his own pain? Concern for his comrades? Or both?

I paused for several moments, hoping he believed I was considering his offer. Then I spun abruptly and stalked toward him. "Very well. If you insist."

"No." Gregor yanked against his chains, attempting to protect his master but failing.

When I reached Mikkel, I held the torch up to shed more light upon him. One of his eyes was nearly swollen shut with purple and blue surrounding the puffy skin. His other cheek was bruised too, likely from Irontooth's fist. Both sleeves were saturated with blood and stuck to his arms. The front of his tunic was smeared with blood, from the cuts on his arms or elsewhere I couldn't determine.

There was only one way to find out.

I lodged the torch into a wall holder, set the bag of supplies down, then slid my knife from its sheath. I held it out, letting the light glint off the sharp blade. I kept my attention focused on Mikkel's face, gauging his emotions. Was he afraid of me and what I could do to him?

Even battered as he was, he was still handsome, perhaps more so now that I'd seen his kindness and consideration toward Gregor and Fowler. Certainly more so than any noblemen I'd ever met.

He didn't look at the knife but leaned his head back against the wall, his body as relaxed—or as much as possible with his arms spread out and manacled to the crevice where the floor and wall met. His position might not be entirely comfortable, but at least I'd spared him having his arms chained to the wall above his head.

I shifted the knife closer to him. And still he ignored it. Instead, he studied my face—what was visible of it above my veil. "So, will you tell me your real name?"

I slid the knife to the drawstring of his tunic at his collarbone. "I shall question you, my lord. Not the other way around."

"Then begin the inquiry."

If he'd had his arms free, I suspected he would have crossed them behind his head. He was too calm. Didn't he believe I was capable of harming him if I so chose?

I thrust the irritation aside. All my life I'd had to be

careful about letting my feelings rule me—whether jealousy or pride or anxiety. I'd watched those emotions control my mother, taking over and turning her into a cruel and vindictive woman at times. I didn't want to become like her. Ever. But was I fated to resemble her regardless of my desire to be different?

In fact, this taunting him with a knife was too similar to my mother's tactics. I needed to pull back and do what I'd come to do—tend his wounds. Yet as I started to lift my knife away, his eyes seemed to mock me, as if to say I didn't have the wherewithal to carry through on torturing him.

I hadn't planned to torture him—had just wanted to scare him a little. But at his challenge, I paused. Then with a flick of my wrist, I cut away the drawstrings on his tunic.

The light in his eyes remained, daring me to do more.

He needn't dare me. I'd do so willingly. Careful to connect just with the fabric and not his skin, I slid my knife down, slicing it wide open and revealing a lighter, thinner tunic underneath. The material was of fine silken quality, belonging to nobility and not a pauper. Nevertheless, he must shed it along with the top garment to give me access to his wounds.

I wrenched upward and rent the material so the ripping echoed in the chamber. Behind me, Gregor's chains rattled as he strained against them. I made another quick slice, cutting first one sleeve loose at the shoulder and then the other. Finally, using the tip of the knife, I tugged the bloodstained linen away.

His tunics in tatters around him, Mikkel still hadn't moved, still reclined against the wall, as if he made an everyday occurrence of sitting in dungeons, facing women wielding knives.

With his arms and chest now bare, his wounds were visible, but blood covered much of his skin and would need to be washed away before I could examine the extent of his injuries.

I stood and returned to the ladder. "I am ready for the last item," I called up to Tommy.

A moment later, he lowered a blackened pot with steam rising up from the water within. As I knelt beside Mikkel and opened the satchel, I avoided his gaze. He'd likely figured out by now that I hadn't come to torture him.

I dipped a rag into the pot, wrung out the excess water, and then gently laid the cloth against his arm upon one of the gashes.

He sucked in a breath and his body jerked against the chains.

I removed the cloth and then dug through my supplies until I found the flask I'd placed there. As I pulled it out and uncorked it, Mikkel shook his head. "No, I don't need anything."

"'Tis but a concoction of wine and theriac and will take the edge off your pain."

"I shall endure the pain without it."

"As I shall need to suture several of your gashes, I insist you drink a little." I lifted the flask to his mouth.

He pressed his lips together and jutted his chin, his light-blue eyes flashing with a determination that was gallant and yet foolhardy.

"Come now." I touched it to his lips again. "Surely with your keen observation skills, you realize that if I wanted you to suffer, I would have refrained from coming to your aid at the outset of the gauntlet."

He shifted his head away from the medicine. "With my *keen observation skills*, I see that you would do whatever Irontooth asks, even if you must slice me open further."

I sat back on my heels, my ire rising once more. "I am my own person and do not bow to Irontooth's every whim."

"'Tis clear enough you allow him to think for you."

"'Tis clear you've forgotten I stood up to Irontooth and gained you an extra week of life."

"So that you might glean private insights into my life to relay to Irontooth."

My irritated retort died upon my lips. Was Mikkel correct in saying I did whatever Irontooth asked, even allowing him to think for me? I'd assumed I'd merely given him my allegiance after he'd taken me in and offered me protection. Somewhere along the way, had I lost sight of who I was? What if I'd never known myself to begin with? After all, I'd lived in the shadows of my mother's demands, answering her call whenever she commanded me.

"Irontooth only wishes to protect me and all the others in our camp." Certainly I hadn't exchanged one dictator for another. Irontooth was nothing like my mother. He cared about me more in the short time I'd known him than my mother had my entire life.

"So you admit you would like me to drink the theriac to loosen my tongue and enable you to report back to Irontooth all he wishes to know about me?"

"I had not thought of that. But 'tis a brilliant plan." I lifted the flask again. Perhaps such a strategy would be easier than winning his affection.

He twisted away from me.

I chased his lips, but he angled farther out of reach, giving me full view of his profile and the awful bruises on his cheek.

I released an exasperated sigh. "You are a stubborn man."

"Thank you, my lady."

"'Twas not a compliment." If he refused to dull the pain, then so be it. I'd let him suffer through my ministrations. I picked up the rag and pressed it to the burn mark.

He hissed through his teeth before he clamped his mouth closed and shut his eyes.

I lightened the pressure. "Daft is a better word—a word you cannot misconstrue for a compliment."

He didn't respond this time, likely in too much pain to think of a retort. As I resumed washing the wounds, I attempted to be careful, but with each touch, he stiffened until his body and limbs were as rigid as the cave walls. Before suturing the first cut in his arm, I offered the medicine again, but he pressed his lips into a hard, straight line.

"Daft," I whispered again. But even as I slipped the needle through his flesh, my admiration for him swelled. He might be foolish, but he exuded a strength unlike any man I'd ever known.

Maybe I'd been amiss to think I could sway him into revealing the truth about his being on the island. What if he didn't tell me anything by the week's end? And what would I do if Irontooth insisted on killing him?

I pushed away the thought. I had seven days to earn Mikkel's trust. Surely I could accomplish the feat if I set my mind to it.

Chapter 5

MIKKEL

FIRE RACED UP AND DOWN MY ARMS AS IF SOMEONE WERE roasting me alive. I jerked to free myself, but I was trapped in the flames. I lurched again, and this time cold shackles dug into my flesh, waking me from one nightmare and plunging me into another as the memories of my capture came back to me.

"How do you fare, Your Highness?" a voice whispered through the thick darkness.

"Gregor." I fought off the pain in order to think clearly. "You're delusional to call me by so great a title."

"Fowler's gone, Your Highness. It's just us."

I relaxed against the cave wall, pressing against a cloak someone had draped around my body. Although my arms and chest burned from my wounds, the rest of my body was cold from the dampness of the cave, and I was grateful for the covering.

My mind scrambled to remember everything that had happened. But my last memory was of the veiled woman stitching my wounds. "How long have I been unconscious?"

"Only a couple of hours."

"What happened to Fowler?"

"They took him up above."

"Is he free?"

"No, he's been made a slave."

I'd expected as much, since enslaving prisoners was the practice over in Blade's camp. What I hadn't counted on was raising their suspicions to the point that they would consider killing me.

At least I had a week to figure out how to keep myself and Gregor alive. What other tale could I spin? I'd already used the most plausible one and had no other ideas. Perhaps I needed to put my energy into devising an escape instead.

I tested my manacles, twisting and turning them.

"I've already tried to free myself," Gregor said. "I can't do it without a knife."

"The one in your sole?"

"I took it out during the gauntlet and couldn't get it back into my boot in time."

The king's weapons master had given us each knives to wear in secret compartments in the soles of our boots. Unfortunately, someone had stolen my boots early in our journey, and I'd had to make do with an old pair I'd purchased after offering myself as a laborer for hire.

Now that both Gregor and I had lost our concealed knives, we'd have a harder time liberating ourselves from our chains. Perhaps we would have to persuade one of the guards to aid us.

The scraping of the door overhead was followed by a slant of light that illuminated the cavern, revealing Gregor chained to the wall opposite me. His scarred face contained bruises like mine, but otherwise he appeared unharmed.

As the ladder descended, I realized that even if we happened to obtain a utensil that might unlock our manacles, we still would need the help of one of the guards to break free of the dungeon. And yet how could we convince any of them when we had nothing to exchange?

Dainty boots stepped onto the first rung and then the second. The veiled woman was coming back. Though her hose and breeches were mostly shielded by the long tunic she wore, I could still see too much of her shapely legs. As she climbed down and hopped to the ground, I tore my attention from her legs to the baskets looped over each arm. The waft of fish soup sent my stomach into a rolling growl.

She lifted her torch higher in my direction. "I see you're finally awake."

"Just in time."

"Just in time for more doctoring?" Her tone contained a hint of teasing that seemed to lighten her eyes.

"Yes, that's exactly what I've been waiting for—more needles digging through my flesh."

She laughed, and the sound was soft and lilting behind her veil. I wished suddenly that I could see the way her lips curved up when she smiled. As though sensing my scrutiny, she dropped her gaze to one of her baskets.

Was it possible I could convince this woman to aid our escape? I sat up straighter, the prospect giving me renewed energy. Already she'd shown her willingness to help us. And she'd just laughed at my weak attempt at jesting. Could I make this woman like me enough in one week that she'd free us?

With her blemishes, perhaps she'd never had much flattery from men. And perhaps she'd relish having someone pay her attention. Such a strategy was worth a try, wasn't it?

As she hooked the torch into the wall, I observed her more carefully. Her dark hair hung in a single thick braid down her back. The curve of a delicate ear showed above the veil as did the arch of a high cheekbone. Her long lashes and narrow brows served to highlight her stunning green eyes.

At one time, she'd likely been an exceptionally beautiful woman, which made her blemishes all the more tragic. No nobleman would ever be able to marry a woman with deformities, regardless of how much he might care for her. He would put himself and his family in danger of becoming an outcast with her.

As she placed the baskets on the floor, my mind spun with the various methods I could employ for winning her affection. A part of my conscience warned against using her this way. But another part whispered that a little wooing would be harmless if doing so could preserve Gregor's and my lives.

"My lady." I tried to make my tone serious. "I am truly grateful for your doctoring."

She knelt beside me and gently peeled back the cloak.

"Without your tender ministrations, my wounds would be festering by now."

She bent closer and examined one of the cuts on my arm.

Think. I'd interacted with many maidens over the past few years as I'd come of age. Wealthy noblemen and foreign kings alike had flaunted their daughters before my brothers and me at court. I'd never been without attention from one comely woman or another. What had I done then to gain their favor?

For a long moment, I scoured the far corners of my brain but could come up with nothing. In all truth, I'd never had to do anything, because the young ladies had been the ones to throw themselves at me.

I glanced sideways at the veiled woman. How could I charm her when I had no idea how to do so? What would Vilmar do if he were in my place? Or Kresten? My youngest brother had been the most winsome amongst the ladies.

I pictured Kresten winking and teasing, tossing back his handsome head and laughing. He'd always been smooth-tongued, saying just the right words to melt a woman's heart. I'd scoffed at his use of such tactics, but what I wouldn't give to have his ability at this moment.

"And how are the wounds feeling?" She bent to examine another of the areas she'd stitched.

What could I say that would sound witty and impressive? The cogs within my mind whirred, but again, I was speechless.

She sat back, her brows furrowing. "That bad, my lord?"

"No, they're doing well enough." I felt suddenly like an awkward lad using a blunt sword instead of a full-grown man on the cusp of ruling a nation.

"Then the poultice I packed into each is easing the pain?"

"Poultice?" I glanced down at my arm and chest to the places she'd stitched. I caught a whiff of spices I couldn't begin to name. "The wounds do hurt, but I'm sure without your efforts I'd have no relief."

She studied another one of the areas and then draped the cloak back over my shoulders and arms. Ought I mention how appealing I looked without my tunic? Vilmar or Kresten would say such a thing.

But somehow the words stuck, and I knew if I forced them, I'd sound even more like an awkward lad.

"You are hungry, are you not?" She reached into one of the baskets and removed a small crock.

"Very."

She lifted the lid and held it close to my face, letting the waft of steam rise beneath my nose.

I attempted to raise my hands to take the bowl from her, only to remember they were securely fastened to the floor. Her eyes lit, almost as if she was smiling in enjoyment at my helplessness.

She rose, crossed to Gregor, and handed him the bowl. Since his hands were free, he took the soup eagerly and began to drink it. Surely she wouldn't be so cruel as to make me watch Gregor eat without giving me anything.

As she returned to the basket and retrieved a second crock, she caught me watching her. "You did not suppose I would let you go hungry, did you?"

"Alas, I confess, it crossed my mind."

"I am not so heartless as that."

"If you're not heartless, then you will unshackle my hands so I might eat like a man and not an animal."

"I would never allow you to eat like an animal, my lord." Her voice was low, and her stunning green eyes captured and held mine as she walked over and knelt next to me. She situated herself, her knees brushing against me. And then she lifted the bowl to my lips, never once averting her eyes. Instead, the green turned dark and seemed to beckon me.

My heart began to thud an unsteady rhythm. When the bowl tipped higher and our connection was lost, I sipped but didn't taste anything. I could only ponder how pretty and expressive her eyes were.

When I finished drinking the last of the soup, she set the bowl on the cave floor and then lifted her hand. Her fingers hovered above my mouth for an eternal second before she dabbed at the corner with her thumb. "You have a drop of soup . . ."

At her touch, something warm streamed into my veins, reminding me of drinking hot glogg on a snowy winter day. The sensation was new, even pleasurable, and something I could welcome.

She retracted her hand, as if stroking my mouth wasn't something she'd planned. And she ducked her head almost shyly before she reached back into the basket and took out another item. A wedge of cheese.

"Would you like more to eat, my lord?"

Was she planning to feed me every meal all week long? How would I endure such sweet torture? And yet how could I say no?

In answer to her question, I opened my mouth.

She broke off a piece of cheese and set it inside, careful not to touch my mouth again. As I chewed, she tore off another portion. "Why is a young man like you yet unmarried? Surely you have had many women vying after you."

"I have been waiting for my father to choose my bride."

"And he has yet to find someone suitable?"

"He's considering several options."

Her brows arched. "Several?"

I smiled. "Is that so surprising, my lady, that several women might be interested in me?"

"Of course not. You are a handsome and brave man."

Her words sent warmth through my middle again,

especially when she dropped her gaze, as if her admission embarrassed her.

I swallowed the cheese, and when she offered another piece, she was again careful not to let her fingers brush my mouth. "Will you get a say in your bride? Or must you accept whomever your father chooses?"

The Lagting and my father were in the process of arranging brides for my brothers and me. They would assign us our marriage partners based on the outcome of the Testing, and we would have no input into the matter. Whoever was awarded the honor of becoming the next king would likely wed the eldest daughter of the King of the Danes—at least that was my speculation. The union would be advantageous for Scania. And the two who weren't chosen as king would marry other princesses.

But I could say none of this. "'Tis of no consequence to me who is chosen for my bride. I trust my father and shall marry the woman he selects for me."

"Then you need not love her?"

"Love? Of course not. My emotions are not important in so great a matter. Surely as a noblewoman you understand that."

She fidgeted with a piece of cheese. "I should like to think even if love is not present initially that it would grow."

"Love can always grow. 'Tis a choice we make to respect and cherish someone."

"Then you disregard feelings of attraction altogether?"

Heretofore, I'd never met a woman who snared my attention for long—at least long enough that I'd felt any sort of attraction worth pursuing. What would have been the point? "Perhaps after I am married I may enjoy the luxury of fostering love and attraction. But at the start, any sort of arrangement would be purely practical."

"You are such a romantic, my lord." Her voice gently scolded me even as she slanted a look my way that fanned warmth through my veins once more. What was it about this woman that made me react in so strange a manner?

"What about you?" I needed to change the subject. "Do you have hope for love?"

She hesitated, staring at the remaining cheese in her hands.

At once, I wished I could take the question back. Of course she didn't have any hope of love, not with her blemishes. "Forgive me for asking. You likely had to give up much when you came to live here."

"My mother never mentioned any marriage plans for me. Perhaps she never intended for me to have a future."

Her mother? "Then your father is gone?"

She nodded, her eyes filling with shadows. "He died three years ago from a heart attack." As she settled next to me and finished feeding me the cheese, I could see from the tense way she held herself that her grief was raw and her love still deep.

We talked of our fathers for some time, reminiscing and sharing fond memories. Finally, the guard above called down to her, and she stood and began to repack the baskets. I didn't want her to go. Strangely enough, the more I talked with her, the more I wanted to keep conversing.

When she started up the ladder, I was tempted to call her back and ply her with more questions. Not because I wanted to use her in escaping, but because I genuinely was interested in knowing more about her.

No matter what physical imperfections she might

have, she was an intriguing woman. And once the door above closed and darkness descended, I already anticipated her next visit.

Chapter 6

Pearl

Over the next week, I spent hours upon hours down in the dungeon with Mikkel tending his wounds, changing bandages, refreshing poultices, and conversing about a wide variety of topics including politics, philosophy, history, and even religion.

Not only was he well educated, but he reflected deeply on matters and had a wealth of wisdom to add to almost any subject. I'd never had such thorough and thoughtful discussions with anyone before, and I enjoyed my time with him, even making additional excuses for why I needed to descend into the dungeon.

Whenever Irontooth or Felicity questioned the appropriateness of my spending so much time with our prisoner, I reminded them Gregor sat a dozen feet away chaperoning us. And, of course, Tommy or one of the other outcasts guarded the entrance and likely heard our conversations as well.

Besides, Irontooth had given me just a week in which to learn Mikkel's purpose on the island, and I endeavored to make the most of every minute to befriend him and gain his trust. Yet, for all my attempts to elicit more information about his deeper motives, he always held back.

Of course, I withheld from him as well, although the better I knew him, the more I wanted to confide in him. On some level, I sensed he would do me no harm. But at the same time, I'd learned I had to be careful whom I trusted. After all, if my own mother could betray me, anyone could.

On the sixth night of captivity, Irontooth commanded workers to prepare a pyre of wood in readiness for burning Mikkel and Gregor. I halted beside Irontooth in front of the growing stacks, trying not to show my dismay. "I thought we were feeding our prisoners to Loch Ness."

Irontooth crossed his arms and glowered at me. "I changed my mind."

I didn't want the prisoners to perish either way. But at least in the sea, they'd have a fighting chance of escaping. "Give me a few more days.

"You've had long enough. Tomorrow they die."

With increasing desperation, I descended into the dungeon, carrying what could very well be Mikkel's and Gregor's last meal.

Earlier in the week, I'd felt guilty for keeping Mikkel so heavily bound and had Tommy unshackle his hands. Now while he ate, my mind spun. I needed to increase my efforts at getting him to talk, even if that meant I must bind him again and scare him with threats.

As soon as I entertained the prospect, I tossed it aside. He was too strong a man to capitulate under duress. He'd shown that by never once taking any of the pain medicine I offered.

From what I could tell, he had no weaknesses I could exploit. Not even a weakness for women.

When he finished his soup, he accepted my offering of bread, cheese, and ale. "You're quiet tonight." He paused in chewing to study me.

"'Tis your last night. Irontooth prepares to burn you at the stake on the morrow."

"Has it already been a week?" He resumed eating, his expression unruffled.

Kneeling beside him, I sat back on my heels. "If you do not believe he will kill you, then you are wrong."

Mikkel finished the last bite of bread, took a drink, and then leaned his head back. "Will my death cause you sorrow?"

There was something likeable about this man. And no matter his reasons for coming to the island, I couldn't condone his death.

Mikkel's accusation from earlier in the week came back to haunt me, the one about being under Irontooth's control. Did I dare defy our daunting leader and insist he spare Mikkel and Gregor? But how could he spare them? Not when the other outcasts expected him to carry through with his word.

"Will you be sad to leave me, my lord?" I countered with a question as I oft did, forcing him to respond first.

"My lady, do you want the truth?" Though his posture was relaxed, his eyes swung to me, the light blue piercing straight to my heart, unsettling me and making my pulse patter faster.

"And what is the truth?"

He brushed back a loose strand of my hair, and the gentleness was nearly my undoing. "You are an amazing woman and have made this last week of my life one of the best weeks of my life."

The sincerity in his tone and expression were more than I could comprehend. Did he truly mean that?

"Yes," he whispered, brushing back another strand. "I mean every word."

How could he read my thoughts so easily? I couldn't keep from leaning into his touch, and I had the urge to reach out and stroke his cheek.

He glanced over to Gregor, and I did likewise. The servant had finished his dinner and was resting with his eyes closed, as though attempting to give us a moment of privacy.

Mikkel turned his attention back to me. "Thank you for being here with me and showing me kindness, though you had no need to do so." With one hand, he stroked my forehead. With his other, he slipped his fingers around mine.

The contact on both fronts set to flight a flock of finches in my stomach. "Since you have been honest, then I shall admit to the truth as well."

"And what is that, my lady?"

"Yes, I shall mourn your death."

His beautiful eyes held mine and searched my soul. I held my breath, hoping he'd see there what he was looking for. When he tugged my hand a moment later and drew me closer, I went to him willingly, settling against his side into the crook of his arm. I was careful not to brush his injuries, although most were healing well and not troubling him any longer. Even the bruises on his face had begun to fade.

He situated me, cradling me with one arm and still holding my hand with his other. I was so close to him, I could feel his warmth along with every rippling muscle in his body. Though I'd had more than my share of flattery and attention from men at court, I'd never felt this close to anyone before. And I couldn't abide the thought that he would perish.

Maybe if I revealed some of the details about my situation, he'd open up about his. And maybe in doing so, I could glean enough to satisfy Irontooth.

I stared at his long fingers wrapped around mine, such strong fingers compared to my delicate ones. With my opposite hand, I tentatively touched him, tracing a path across his hand to his wrist, to his arm.

I felt him tremble—or at least I thought I did. His reaction gave me an ounce of courage. "Mikkel . . ."

The warmth of his breath against my temple sent the birds inside me fluttering once more. "Yes, my lady?"

I closed my eyes and reveled in the sensation but blurted the words before I changed my mind. "My real name is Pearl."

He was silent for a heartbeat, as though digesting my revelation. What if he'd heard the name before in association with Warwick and Princess Pearl? As my fear mounted, I tried to silence it. Even if he had heard of Princess Pearl, he would assume, like the rest of the world, that the princess died last year in a hunting accident.

"It's a beautiful name," he whispered. "And it suits you."

I released a tense breath I hadn't known I was holding and relaxed into him. "I have always hated the name." It reminded me too much of Warwick's jewels and the gem mines and how consumed my mother was with gaining wealth.

"I have seen the beautiful woman you are on the inside. And that is truly what matters most."

He'd misunderstood me. He assumed I was deformed and that's why I hated my name. Should I tell him I had no blemish and didn't belong on the island any more than he did?

"Thank you, Mikkel." Uncertainty welled within me. Irontooth wouldn't want me to reveal it. As a condition for remaining on the island, he'd insisted I wear the veil at all times and let everyone assume I was deformed. If the other outcasts learned I had no blemish—was in fact known for my beauty—they'd despise me, perhaps even harm me.

"I mean it." His whisper was warm against my temple.

I curled closer into his side.

At the gentle pressure of his lips against my head, I stilled, my whole body tingling with awareness of this man, of his strength, determination, intelligence, and sweetness. I couldn't deny any longer that my attraction to him had been steadily growing. His kiss might be purely platonic, and he might not have any desire for me beyond friendship, but I liked him ... much more than I ought to.

"You can tell me what happened to your face," he said softly. "It won't change how I see you."

"Yes, it will."

"I vow it won't."

I paused. Maybe I couldn't take off my veil and show him my fairness, but I could tell him who I really was, couldn't I? If I did so, would he finally share who he was? "Mikkel?"

"Hmmm . . .?"

"I am—a princess."

Chapter 7

MIKKEL

I FROZE. PEARL WAS A PRINCESS?

"My mother is Queen Margery of Warwick." She whispered the queen's name as if speaking of a deadly plague.

"Truly?"

She nodded, tightening her fingers within mine, but not before I caught the tremor that told me far more than her words—telling me about her background made her feel vulnerable and frightened.

But why?

I scrambled to remember all I knew about Queen Margery and her children. Though I'd never had the opportunity to meet Warwick's queen and family, I made a point of keeping abreast of Scania's relationships with the surrounding nations. And nothing I'd heard about Warwick and Queen Margery had been pleasant.

Early in her reign of Warwick, she'd been obsessed with hunting down her niece, Queen Aurora, who was heir to Mercia's throne. Because of Margery's determination to eliminate the young queen, Aurora had been hidden away, and her father was serving as regent until she reached an age when she could reign in her own right.

After years of searching, Margery seemed to have given up her aspirations of taking the throne from her niece. I guessed the time was soon coming when Aurora would come out of hiding and that perhaps Margery would attempt to destroy her niece again.

Several years ago, we'd learned that Margery's husband had died. And last summer, hadn't we received news that her oldest daughter had perished? In a hunting accident?

Ethelbard was the name of the queen's son. That I knew because he would someday be a rival king. But I hadn't paid attention to the names of Margery's daughters. Something to do with jewels? Perhaps Pearl had been one of them.

"Margery's oldest daughter died," I said. "So you are her youngest child?"

"No, I am her firstborn. Though she tried to kill me during a hunting expedition, one of the huntsmen helped me escape. I ran away and have been living here ever since."

If an illness or accident had compromised Pearl's beauty, then she would no longer be a valuable asset to the queen in brokering an advantageous marriage. In fact, maybe Pearl had posed an embarrassment and burden, one the queen wished to eliminate.

"I have heard of Margery's cruelty. But I didn't think she was so evil that she would kill her own daughter."

Pearl started to pull away. "You do not believe me?"

"I do believe you." I drew her back, not ready for this moment of closeness to come to an end. "I am confused why she would do such a thing, 'tis all."

"Then we shall be confused together." The deep echo of hurt in Pearl's voice told me that she had indeed suffered at the hand of the queen.

I tried to digest everything Pearl had just revealed. She was royalty. Now the conversations we'd had over the past week made more sense. I'd marveled at her enlightenment of matters having to do with ruling a country as well as her insights into other issues that most noble-women wouldn't concern themselves with. She was educated beyond what was normal for nobility, and she also carried herself with a proud bearing.

I relaxed against the cold stone wall. "Princess Pearl."

"Shh," she whispered. "Please do not speak of my identity to anyone else."

"If you wish."

"Vow it." Her tone took on the commanding quality I'd heard from time to time, and now I understood why. She squeezed my hand. "Please, Mikkel."

"Very well. I vow it."

"Irontooth and Felicity are the only ones here in camp who know who I am. And Irontooth will be angry if he learns I have told you."

"Then he fears I'm here as a spy for the queen?"

"He is a good leader, but he worries about everything."

"He need not worry. I'm not here to do you any harm. In fact, once upon a time, Queen Margery had sought an alliance and asked my father about the possibility of a marriage between the Princess Pearl and the next Scanian king." With Warwick's dwindling resources and growing poverty, the Lagting had decided against forging such a union. "Just think, if things had turned out differently, we may have married each other."

At Pearl's stiffening and Gregor's exasperated sigh, I realized I'd said too much.

"It wouldn't have happened." I tried to think of a way to cover my mistake. "The king of Scania is more interested in the princess of the Danes as a future wife for his heir—"

"And you are the next heir?" she asked quietly.

"No, no. The heir is determined by a process of Testing."

"So you came to the island for your Testing?"

Denial pushed against my tongue. But how could I lie to her when she'd told me the truth about who she was?

"So you are a prince of Scania. And you have two brothers, do you not?"

Again, I held myself back. It was one thing to divulge my identity and put my Testing at risk. But I couldn't jeopardize the Testing for Vilmar and Kresten.

She pulled away, and this time I let her. She didn't go far, only pivoted so she was kneeling and facing me.

A cold shiver worked its way up my spine. I hadn't intended to reveal my true purpose for being on the island. How had this happened? "Please, I beg of you. Do not speak of this to anyone. As you have wanted to keep your identity hidden, I do as well."

She studied my face as though seeing me for the first time. "Is revealing your identity against the rules of the Testing?"

"Already everyone rejects me for being different than them. If they discover I am a prince, they'll kill me. And if not, they'll banish me from the island and never allow me back. If that happens, I shall forfeit any chance at gaining the kingship."

"Prince Mikkel." She tested my name. "You are the firstborn son of King Christian of the Holbergs."

I didn't deny her, but neither could I openly admit to it.

"I should have guessed as much." She rose and reached for the empty food basket.

"Vow you will keep my secret the same as I vowed to keep yours."

She took a step backward toward the ladder. "Which is more important—your life or your Testing?"

"My Testing." I would rather lose my life than fail at my Testing. At least then I would die with honor.

Once again she examined me, her keen eyes seeming to see deep inside to my soul. Finally, she shook her head and reached for the ladder. "I am sorry, Mikkel. But I cannot stand by and watch you die when it is within my power to save you."

"I didn't ask for you to save me."

"You will thank me later."

I sat forward, needing to go to her and somehow talk reason into her. "I can fend for myself."

"And that is what you have done this past week?"

"Yes, I have been biding my time."

"And now you have run out."

I glanced toward the opening above and then lowered my voice. "Help me escape."

Her eyes narrowed.

"Next time you come down, bring a pin or knife or something sharp we can use to pick our locks. Then you can distract the guard above while we sneak away."

"You wish for me to betray my friends?"

"Are we not friends now too?"

She hesitated, her eyes turning a murky green. "This

past week you befriended me so you could use me to aid in your escape?"

Perhaps I'd started with ulterior motives, but I'd genuinely grown to like her. "I hoped you might be willing to aid me, but our interactions became more than that."

"More?" Her voice rose a notch. "How grand of you."

The conversation was rapidly deteriorating. I needed to redeem myself. But how? "You cannot deny you befriended me this week so you could discover the reason for my presence on the island." As soon as the words were out, I saw them as the excuse they were. But it was too late to retract them.

"Yes, you are correct. I came down here tonight intending to find a way to get information from you."

"Then you told me who you were with the hope I would do the same?"

She lifted her shoulders and tilted up her chin.

A knot tightened in my gut. She didn't have to say anything more for me to know the truth. She'd been using me all week. And though I had no reason to be upset at her, since I was likewise guilty, the revelation stung nevertheless.

"Now I suppose you will run to Irontooth with everything you've learned about me." I couldn't keep the bitterness from my tone.

She grasped a rung on the ladder. "At least in doing so, I shall save your life."

"And ingratiate yourself to your leader."

Without another glance my way, she began climbing up.

With each step she took, I saw my chances of succeeding at the Testing slipping away. I needed to call after her, beg her to come back, apologize profusely, and attempt to speak with her more calmly.

Vilmar would have known just what to say to talk his way out of the predicament. And charming Kresten wouldn't have gotten himself cornered to begin with. But I could only watch Pearl ascend, frustration swirling inside and making me mute.

She was as much to blame for what had happened as I was, wasn't she? She'd curled up next to me like a kitten and coaxed me until I'd said everything she wanted to hear.

I wouldn't apologize. Not when she'd so blatantly beguiled me into revealing more than I should have.

As she disappeared and the hatch slammed shut, Gregor released another sigh. "That went well, Your Highness."

"Yes, very."

With Pearl's torch remaining in the wall holder and illuminating the cave, I could see Gregor retrieving the journal and charcoal writing stub he kept hidden within an inner pocket of his tunic.

Of course he would take advantage of the light to add to his records, as he tried to do most days. At the end of the six months, he would hand the journal to the Lagting and my father so they could read an account of everything that happened during the Testing.

I didn't begrudge him the light and the need to write about what had just transpired between Pearl and me. He was doing his job as he should. The question was, could I still find a way to continue with my Testing even after everyone on the island learned I was a prince?

I shook my head, frustration burning in my gut. Was there anything—anything at all—I could do to salvage the situation?

Chapter 8

Pearl

"Say it again." Irontooth's silver brows arched high, showing his surprise.

At a movement outside, I glanced to the cave opening and gauged who might be listening to our conversation. The darkness of the coming night had settled, and most of the outcasts had gathered around the central fire pit for dinner and conversation.

Though part of me was angry enough at Mikkel that I didn't care who heard the revelation, my guilt warred fiercely enough inside that I'd requested a private meeting with Irontooth.

Felicity ducked through the entrance. "Just me." Her pale face reflected the same gravity she'd shown the day I revealed my identity, telling me she'd just been listening. She closed the door behind her and then crossed to stand beside Irontooth.

"Go on." Irontooth nudged a loose log in the hearth that gave low light to the cave, which consisted of naught more than sleeping pallets and weapons.

"Mikkel is Prince Mikkel Holberg," I said again, my voice still low, "son of King Christian of the great kingdom of Scania."

Irontooth whistled between his iron-tipped teeth. "A prince."

"He's here for a Testing his country demands of him, a Testing that determines which son is worthy of becoming the next king."

"How long does he need to stay?"

"I do not know. He did not say." I'd been lucky to get what I had from him. And now he hated me because of the deception . . . if he'd ever liked me to begin with. Perhaps all along he'd been repelled by my veil and the blemish he believed I had.

"This means I cannot kill him," Irontooth said.

"Not unless you want to make an enemy of Scania."

Irontooth stared into the flames, no doubt weighing his options of what to do with this unwanted prince.

"Send him back to Scania." Although Mikkel had revealed how much he wanted to remain and finish his Testing, I was too hurt by his betrayal to care. He'd made clear enough that his Testing was more important than anything else, including friendship.

My stomach pinched at the thought that he'd been pretending to be my friend. He'd used me all week. The fascinating conversations, the deep discussions, the hours of debating—it had all been for one purpose: to win my trust so in the end, I'd be willing to do his bidding and set him free.

"Sending him home prematurely will result in his disgrace," I explained. "He'll have to forfeit the kingship."

"And if he stays?"

"Everyone already despises him. If word gets out

that he is a prince, they will kill him."

"True."

"At the very least they will cast him off the island and ban him from coming back."

"So." Felicity sidled closer to Irontooth and slid her arm through his. "We now have both a princess and a prince on our island. I cannot help but think Providence has a hand in this."

"Mikkel cannot stay." I didn't want to see him again. In fact, the sooner he was sent away, the better.

"You seemed to like him." Felicity raised a pale eyebrow.

"I loathe him."

"That is not what I observed. In fact, you seemed quite suited for each other." From the gleam in Felicity's eyes, I guessed she'd listened at the dungeon door to my conversations with Mikkel, perhaps spied on us for Irontooth.

"He was using me to help him escape."

"And you were using him to gain information."

I couldn't deny it, but somehow his betrayal seemed worse. After all, he'd chosen me, thinking I was a vulnerable and damaged young woman he could make feel special. As handsome as he was, he'd likely felt sorry for me and believed he'd have no trouble winning my favor.

"So what should I do with our prisoner?" Irontooth asked.

"You should keep him on the island," Felicity said.

"Send him back to Scania," I said at the same moment.

Irontooth glanced between us and crossed his arms, his eyes narrowing.

"We have been wondering how to keep Pearl safe

from the queen long term," Felicity murmured to him. "We've wanted to find a good home for her. Now one has been dropped into our lap."

"I have been safe enough here."

Irontooth shot me a glare that warned me he was losing his patience. I bit back another remark and deferred to Felicity.

She bowed her head at me. "We'll allow him to stay and will assure him we'll guard his privacy . . . so long as he agrees to take Pearl home with him to Scania when he is done with his Testing."

"No! I shall have nothing more to do with him—"

"Aye, you will," Irontooth snarled. "Now hold your tongue, or I'll hold it for you."

I lifted my chin defiantly. "You know I am leaving the island by summer's end and traveling to Warwick to rescue Ruby."

Felicity rubbed Irontooth's shoulder, her long fingers soothing him. "Now, Pearl, keep in mind, if you go to Scania with a prince, he'll have a much greater chance at bargaining with the queen for Ruby than you will in sneaking in and attempting to kidnap her."

Was that true? If he became king, would he be able to sway the queen to release Ruby into my care? And would she be safest in Scania? Mikkel may have been deceptive this past week, but I couldn't discount his many fine qualities that would serve him well as a king. And living in Scania with Ruby would be better than subjecting her to the perils on the Isle of Outcasts or even running away to the Continent.

"Do you see the wisdom in such a plan, Pearl?" Felicity turned gentle eyes upon me.

"I do not wish to coerce him into taking me to Scania."

"I don't think he'll need coercing by the time his Testing is done." Felicity bestowed upon me a knowing smile. "I'll wager he'll loathe leaving you behind."

"You'll wager in vain."

Felicity bent and whispered in Irontooth's ear. At his grunts, I guessed he was agreeing to her plan. When she pulled back and looked at me again, her smile was pleased, as if she'd just solved a problem that had been worrying her for a long time.

I hadn't realized she and Irontooth had been perplexed about my future or that they'd wanted to find a different place for me to live. Was I putting them and the other outcasts in more peril than I'd realized?

Irontooth crossed the cave floor and opened the door. "Bring me the prisoners from the dungeon!"

I made a move to leave, but he turned and blocked the way, his scowl stopping me more than his big body. "We're not finished here, and you need to stay until we are."

"This is for the best," Felicity added. "You'll see."

I didn't want to encounter Mikkel again, but I guessed I would have to endure one more meeting with him. After that, I would do my best to stay as far away from him as possible.

Mikkel

I didn't resist as the man with the webbed hands, the one called Toad, pushed me to my knees in front of Irontooth.

When he'd shoved me through the door a moment ago, I noticed Pearl standing in the shadows and was grateful to be on my knees so I didn't have to see her expression.

No doubt she was gloating that she'd extracted information from me. And no doubt she'd gone straight to Irontooth with it.

The question was, what would he do to me now that he knew I was a prince?

Gregor tumbled to his knees next to me, his head bent in subservience.

Somewhere in the climb up and walk to the cave, I'd lost the borrowed cloak so that once again, I found myself bare chested in a state of undress. Though I'd been freed from my dungeon manacles, my hands were now chained together behind my back.

As the guards left and closed the door behind them, I waited. If Irontooth forced me to leave the island, perhaps I'd pretend to go willingly but then eventually make my way back to Blade's camp and complete my Testing there.

At once, I cast the idea aside as foolish. Even though Irontooth and Blade were warring against one another, the island was small enough that word of my royalty would spread.

"Prince Mikkel." Scorn dripped from Irontooth's voice. "You came to our island so you could feel better about yourself compared to all of us, is that it?"

I lifted my head and met his gaze across the fire pit. "I came so I could learn to see beyond mere appearances and gain compassion."

"We don't need your compassion."

"Perhaps you don't, but someday the people of Scania will benefit from having a king who understands their weaknesses and can empathize with them rather than look down upon them."

Irontooth's jaw flexed. "Are you saying we're weak?"

"We are all weak in one way or another. It's what we do with our weaknesses that counts."

"And how are you weak?"

I'd always believed I was strong. But the deprivation, uncertainty, threat of danger, and even lack of being accepted had chipped away at my self-confidence, so now I was no longer certain how strong I was.

Was pride my weakness? Was that what my father and the Lagting had hoped my Testing would expose and then strip away?

"I am still learning my weaknesses, and I see more of them with each day I live on the island."

Irontooth was silent for a moment as the albino woman next to him whispered in his ear. I glanced in Pearl's direction. She was staring into the fire, her beautiful eyes flaming with anger.

Was she angry with me? She had no right to be. Perhaps I'd had hidden motives for friendship early on, but that had changed as the week went on and I'd gotten to know her, or at least thought I had, until she'd tricked me into sharing who I was.

"We have decided what to do with you," Irontooth said.

My back stiffened in preparation for the news. Would he kill me or send me away? And which would be better?

"I understand you want to keep your royalty hidden the same way Pearl is hiding hers. Otherwise you will jeopardize your Testing."

Apparently Pearl hadn't withheld anything I'd told her. "Yes, that is true."

Irontooth stared at Pearl, who kept her attention riveted to the fire, before he shifted his brooding gaze back to me. "I won't say anything about who you are, to anyone. And you don't have to leave."

"What?" Pearl's question was loaded with frustration.

Hope sparked inside me, and I shared a look with Gregor. His eyes mirrored my surprise.

"Thank you—"

Irontooth waved his hand impatiently. "There is one condition."

"Very well."

"You must marry Princess Pearl and take her back to Scania as your wife when you are finished here."

"Marry?" Pearl spoke at the same time I did. Except her tone held anger. "That is a ridiculous proposition."

"I concur."

"You said nothing of marrying." She continued to ignore me and directed her glare to Irontooth. "Only of returning with him to Scania."

"How else did you suppose you could travel with him?" the albino woman said kindly. "Surely you know there's no other way it can be done. And surely you know that's the best way of securing Ruby."

Pearl pursed her lips. I guessed Ruby was her younger sister, the one she'd spoken of so fondly from time to time during the last week. Even so, no matter her desperation to escape from the clutches of her mother and find a new home, I couldn't marry her.

"But the law"—Pearl's tone rose—"prevents marriage until the age of twenty, and I am only nineteen. Any marriage made before that is illegal, punishable by death."

"That is the law in Warwick, not here in Norland." Irontooth crossed his arms, the clear sign that he refused to accept any excuse Pearl might offer.

Pearl's forehead creased with panic.

"Law or no," I cut in, "I am not at liberty to get married."

Irontooth glared at me. "Then I'll tell everyone who you really are, and your Testing—possibly your life—will be over."

My mind scrambled to find a way out of this dilemma. "As a prince and the future king, my father and his advisors must determine my bride. They are, in fact, already making arrangements. That is the way of things, and I cannot change it."

"Think nothing of Irontooth's offer," Pearl stated. "I would not marry you even if your father and his advisors asked for my hand."

"You needn't worry." My ire rose much too swiftly. "I don't want to marry you either."

"Good."

"Yes, good." Even if I wanted to marry her, I couldn't make so binding a commitment to a woman who must wear a veil to hide her deformities. My people would never accept her. In fact, many would accuse her of being a witch.

As though seeing the direction of my thoughts, hurt flared within Pearl's eyes. "I would never bind myself to a man who places so much value on outward worth."

"I cannot disregard it—"

"Enough!" Irontooth thundered. "You will wed Pearl, or the deal is off." The look in his eyes told me he was serious.

"Please try to understand . . ."

The silver-haired leader moved away from the fire and stalked to the door.

"This isn't a decision I can make so quickly or lightly." My tone was now laced with desperation.

He reached the door and began to swing it open.

My pulse sped, and I struggled to my feet. "Wait!"

He didn't stop, merely pushed the door wider and shouted outside, "I have an announcement—"

"I'll do it."

With a glance at me over his shoulder, he arched his brows.

"I shall marry her."

"It doesn't matter whether he will or not." Pearl stomped her foot. "I refuse to consider it."

"Do you vow it?" Irontooth asked without glancing at Pearl.

I squelched my trepidation. I would figure a way out of this quandary at some point. For now, making the promise was the only way I could stay on the island and continue my Testing. Moreover, Pearl didn't want to marry me any more than I did her. No matter the vow Irontooth might extract from me, Pearl would refuse to pledge herself to me.

Irontooth turned his attention to the camp and addressed his people again. "I've discovered the ident—"

"I vow it!"

He looked at me as he continued to shout out the door. "I discovered that our prisoner has come to the island for a bride."

A weight settled on my chest.

"You must not say it!" Pearl started toward Irontooth, but the albino woman caught her arm.

"And he's just agreed to marry Veil."

"No." Pearl strained to free herself.

"We'll hold the wedding tonight!" Irontooth finished

with a triumphant smile.

Cheers and whistles rose into the night air.

"Prepare a feast!" he called as more cheers filled the camp.

"No!" Pearl broke loose and rushed toward Irontooth and the door. He swung it shut and spun, catching her as she threw herself at him.

"How dare you?" She swung both fists at his chest.

He easily caught her wrists. "This is for your own good."

She wrestled against him. "I shall determine my fate, not you."

Though I wanted to rush to her aid, I held myself back. Her refusal was my only hope in extricating myself from the vow I'd just given Irontooth.

"The queen won't be able to touch you once you're married."

"I shall fend for myself."

"He's a powerful prince. He'll give you a good home and take care of you."

"You know nothing about him!"

"He took the gauntlet punishment for himself and spared his manservant. That's all I need to know."

The fight eased from Pearl, and she ceased struggling.

I studied Irontooth more carefully. Had he truly intended to kill me on the morrow? Or had he hung the threat over me in order to get me to do his bidding? Perhaps I'd misjudged this leader. Thus far, I considered him nothing more than a savage brute. Was he more cunning than I'd allowed?

"Felicity said he's strong of character, never once complaining about his injuries."

Pearl glanced at my wounds, which she'd doctored all

week. "He is arrogant and untrustworthy."

Arrogant and untrustworthy? I wanted to defend myself, but what if she was right?

"He can give you and Ruby everything you need." The woman crossed to Pearl and touched her shoulder. "And most importantly, he'll keep you both safe from the queen."

"I can keep Ruby safe on my own," Pearl replied, although weakly.

My body tensed with the need to step in and say something, but I suspected my interference would make matters worse. With how much Pearl disliked me, she surely wouldn't capitulate to Irontooth and the woman.

"Sometimes we must make sacrifices for the people we love," the woman continued. "And this is a sacrifice you can make for Ruby—although I suspect with time you won't see it as so much of a sacrifice."

Pearl held herself stiffly for another moment before her shoulders drooped.

The weight in my chest pressed harder. She wouldn't go through with marrying me, would she?

Chapter 9

Pearl

How had the situation spiraled so quickly out of control? I'd only intended to save Mikkel's life . . . and perhaps I'd also hoped to impress Irontooth with my ability to glean the information he wanted from our prisoner.

Nevertheless, I hadn't expected Irontooth and Felicity to insist I marry Mikkel.

Irontooth released my wrists, and Felicity swept me into an embrace, wrapping me solidly in her arms. Though I wanted to be angry at them both, I knew they had my best interests at heart.

If I was honest, I couldn't deny that their plan was brilliant. In fact, if I arrived in Scania without the queen knowing I was alive, Mikkel could invite Ethelbard to visit and encourage him to bring Ruby. Once Ruby was in Scania, the queen would be helpless to get her back. We would be able to live the rest of our lives in peace and safety and comfort.

But could I really marry a man who didn't want me?

I pulled back and looked at Mikkel. He stood beside the fire, the muscles in his bare chest straining against the chains binding his hands behind his back. Gregor had risen to stand next to his master, watching but saying nothing.

The hearth, while not bright, provided enough light for me to catch the glimmer of panic in Mikkel's eyes. This past week, in all our interactions, I had not taken him for the type of man to allow the outward appearance of others to influence his decisions. And yet, here he was, resistant to the thought of marrying a woman with a deformity. Or perhaps he truly feared displeasing his father and the advisors by marrying without their permission.

In either case, I straightened my spine and stood taller, letting his panic strengthen my resolve.

As if sensing my decision, he gave a shake of his head.

I lifted my chin. "I shall marry the prince."

He clenched his mouth closed, his jaw flexing as though he was using great care to hold in his frustration.

Once again, I was tempted to tug off my veil and reveal the truth about my beauty. But he didn't deserve to know, not after spurning me.

"I shall marry him," I said again. "But if the queen discovers I am alive, she must not know I have married the prince—at least, not until after Ruby is by my side in Scania where she will be safe."

Mikkel's chains clanked behind him as if he was struggling to free himself. "Perhaps we can wait to marry until later—"

"No," Irontooth groused. "Today. Now. Before

either of you finds a way to get out of it."

"Then we will stay quiet about the marriage?" I persisted. "No one but those on this island can know."

Mikkel studied me. "You fear if the queen learns you're alive and married to me, then she won't allow Ruby to come to Scania?"

"I fear she could do anything, and I must use extreme caution until I have Ruby away from her."

Irontooth squeezed my shoulder. "You're making the right choice, Pearl. You'll be happy. You'll see."

I nodded, but that didn't mean I agreed with him. I opted instead to concur with Felicity's admonishment to make sacrifices for the people we loved. This marriage wasn't for me. It was for Ruby, to secure a new home for her.

"Now, both of you get ready." All pleasantness left Irontooth's tone. "We'll have the wedding just as soon as we find a tunic for the prince." With that, he swung open the door and ducked outside.

Felicity smoothed a hand over my sleeve. "You'll want to dress in something nicer."

"No, I shall wear what I have on." This wasn't the wedding of my dreams—not that I'd dreamed of a wedding. If I'd entertained such fancy notions, I'd never imagined my nuptials happening this way—in the dark amongst outcasts, to a man who had no desire to wed me.

I started toward the door.

"Pearl," Mikkel said. "Wait."

Something in his voice made me pause. I glanced at him over my shoulder.

"You don't have to do this," he said urgently. "You don't have to let Irontooth dictate what you do."

Did he still believe I was doing Irontooth's every bidding? That I wasn't strong enough to stand up for myself? "I have made up my mind to go through with it. I shall do it for Ruby."

"You don't have to marry me to aid Ruby. Once I have returned to Scania, I shall help you whether we are married or not."

But would he? What motivation would he have to help me then? Why would he after the treatment he'd received thus far on the island?

"This plan was not of my making. But now that it is set into motion, I will not oppose it." Before he could say anything more to sway me, I retreated outside and strode toward the center fire pit and the waiting crowd.

MIKKEL

I stood next to Pearl under the summer night sky, the stars and moon acting as witnesses to our marriage along with two dozen or more outcasts as well as Fowler and Gregor on the periphery of the gathering.

The irony of my circumstances didn't escape me. Only a week earlier, these people had taunted me and tried to kill me as I'd run through the gauntlet, and now they were smiling and wishing me well as I married Pearl.

The priest cleared his throat, drawing my attention back to the ceremony.

"I will," I said.

Titters and guffaws erupted around us.

"I was blessing the ring, my lord." The priest held out a ring amidst the shreds of linen covering his palm. With bandages around his face, hands, and feet, his leprosy was covered, and yet the disease had eaten enough of his flesh that he'd been forced from his monastery and had found sanctuary here on the island.

"The ring." I stared at the simple gold band someone had donated for the occasion.

"It goes on her finger, my lord," the priest said amidst more laughter from the onlookers.

I reached for the band. Once I placed it on Pearl's finger, I'd seal my fate. My mind had been racing ever since Pearl had agreed to marry me. Was there some way I could salvage the situation?

At least she was a princess whom my father and the Lagting had once briefly considered as a possible bride. That could work in my favor. And if I could gain their sympathy for Pearl and Ruby, that might help dispel their anger and disappointment.

At Irontooth's sharp elbow to my ribs, I took the ring and at the same time lifted Pearl's hand. Her fingers were cold beneath mine, and above her veil, her eyes had been frosty throughout the entire ceremony and the stating of our vows.

Though my frustration with her had given way to resignation, she was clearly still angry with me. I slid the ring down and repeated after the priest: "With this ring I thee wed, with my body I thee worship, and with all my worldly goods I thee endow: In the name of the Father, and of the Son, and of the Holy Ghost. Amen."

The priest made the sign of the cross. "Amen."

A murmur of "amens" came from around us.

"I now pronounce that you are man and wife." The

priest smiled broadly.

I couldn't make myself smile in return. Though I couldn't see her mouth beneath her veil, Pearl's severe expression told me she took no joy in our union either.

"Kiss her!" someone shouted at the periphery.

"Kiss yourself!" Pearl shouted back, which earned roaring laughter in response.

In the flickering firelight, her gaze snagged with mine for the first time since we'd stood together at the center of the camp. What was she thinking? That she'd made a big mistake? Because that's what I was thinking.

The words I'd just uttered reverberated in my mind, the promise to worship her with my body and to endow her with my worldly goods. I could easily provide for her every need. But worship her with my body? Could I do that?

Her attention dropped to my mouth before it jumped away.

She wasn't seriously considering their suggestion to kiss, was she? Though we hadn't yet spoken of the nature of our marriage, I suspected she saw it as a business agreement and nothing more.

Moreover, kissing would involve lifting her veil. And that would likely be too embarrassing for her. Although I was curious about the nature of her blemish, I was also somewhat reluctant to witness it. What if it was hideous and changed my view of her for the worse? Perhaps I was better off remaining ignorant.

As the feasting began, thankfully no more was said about kissing. And when the music and dancing started, I stood to the side and watched, my emotions twisting and turning as fast as the dancers, Pearl amongst them. On the one hand, I was grateful to be out of the dungeon and walking around after a week of immobility. I was also relieved I could continue with my Testing.

However, another part of me wondered if I'd failed at my Testing after all, by allowing all of this to happen. I never should have gotten captured in the first place. If I'd been more careful and alert, I'd still be ensconced in Blade's camp, analyzing inner motivations of people and learning more about the human condition as a result. If I'd been more strategic, I would have discovered a way to escape from the dungeon without having to use Pearl. And if I'd been wiser, I would have been able to find a way out of marrying her.

As it was, in spite of my mistakes, I needed to move forward, attempt to redeem myself, and work harder at my Testing. That's what a good leader did. Learn and grow and do better the next time.

By the time people began to nod off, the stars had grown dim and dawn was fast approaching. Nevertheless, a rowdy group of revelers decided to usher us to Pearl's cave that would evidently be my home for the duration of my stay on the island.

Singing at the top of their voices, the group pushed Pearl and me inside the cave and then slammed the door shut behind us. For several minutes, the teasing and songs continued until they faded into yawns and footsteps drifted away.

A strange silence descended within the cave. Pearl stood by the door, facing it, her back stiff. I allowed myself to take stock of her home, noting that it felt homier than Irontooth's. Her furnishings consisted of a sleeping mat with a thick fur blanket, a table and benches made of rocks and boards hewn from the forest, crocks and clay jars, a braided wall hanging, as well as several woven mats surrounding a small fire pit.

"You have crafted a welcoming home," I offered, knowing I needed to put her at ease.

She turned, then, to face me, her eyes flashing with censure. "You must know I am not welcoming you here willingly."

The words had their intended effect. They stung me. But what could I expect? She'd been trapped into marriage to a man she didn't like or know.

She sighed, her breath laced with weariness. "Forgive me. You are not to blame for what has happened. I brought this upon myself."

"I am responsible too." My mind returned to all the things I might have done differently if I'd been a better man. Perhaps Vilmar was the best candidate for king after all. Perhaps this time on the island was laying bare my weaknesses and showing me the truth about myself in a way I'd never before seen.

She crossed to the fire and added another log to the low flames.

"I shouldn't have considered using your friendship to help me gain my freedom. I was selfish and calloused to do so."

"'Twas indeed selfish." She poked at the wood, sending sparks into the air.

"I apologize and pray that with time, you'll be able to forgive me."

She tossed in dry brush, and the flames leapt higher. "I likely would have done the same if our situations had been reversed."

"Then you accept my contrition?"

"I shall, eventually."

"Thank you." As I stared at the flames, the crackling

and warmth of the fire made me drowsy. And yet I needed to persist in making peace with this woman—who was now my wife. "I would have enjoyed the friendship with you even if our situations had been reversed."

My statement had the desired effect. She lifted her eyes to mine, the comely green revealing vulnerability—the same vulnerability I'd seen from time to time during the past week.

"And I would have aided you and Ruby even if we weren't man and wife."

Her eyes flashed with uncertainty, and I guessed she wanted to believe me. But she didn't trust me. Perhaps trust was something one could only earn with time and repeated efforts.

She glanced back to the fire. "I did not trap you into marriage for myself. I did it for Ruby."

"I understand." I prayed my father and the Lagting would understand too.

She was silent a moment before speaking in a low voice. "When Ruby and I are safe from the queen, I would not oppose you if you gave me an annulment. If we remain silent about our marriage, perhaps no one need know about it."

Had she read my thoughts and guessed the difficulties we would face upon returning to Scania? And should I seriously consider her offer? It would make my life easier. And yet, I'd been taught never to make promises I couldn't keep.

"I made vows to both you and Irontooth this night, and I shall not break my word."

"You were coerced."

"I had a choice." One always had a choice, and I'd made mine.

"I shall still give you an annulment."

"And I shall not accept it."

"You must know I do not wish to have a real marriage." She said the words bravely but stared into the fire, refusing to look at me.

"Of course. We shall remain chaste." For now. But I didn't say that. If I became king, I would eventually need to produce an heir. As royalty herself, she would understand such a responsibility. However, I wouldn't trouble myself about that at the moment. At present, it was enough that we could remain civil to each other.

She seemed satisfied with my answer and our truce. "Would you like the pallet or the bearskin blanket?"

"You choose your preference. I shall be satisfied with either."

A few minutes later, we were both lying down on either side of the fire, I upon the pallet and she upon the blanket. She lifted her hands to her veil as though to remove it. But at the sight of my eyes upon her, she turned on her side so she was facing away from the fire.

I studied her outline a moment longer. *Look on the heart.* Though I'd attempted to do so all along with every-one I met on the island, now I had a bigger challenge—to look on the heart of my wife.

My wife. The thought pulsed through me with slug-gish trepidation. Never in all my planning had I expected to end up married on the Isle of Outcasts. But here I was, with a wife. No matter how she might feel about our marriage, I was determined to make the best of it. And in some ways, that might end up being the biggest challenge of all.

Chapter
10

Pearl

"We don't need to fight with Blade," **Mikkel whispered** from where he crouched on the rock ledge beside me.

"We are defending ourselves. Not fighting." I peered down into the gorge, searching for any sign of Blade's men creeping up the river path.

"We would all fare better if we worked together," Mikkel said, as he already had on several occasions. "We would be stronger if we put aside our problems and united."

"We are strong enough," I retorted, my bowstring touching my shoulder and my arrow notched.

He was silent for a moment before whispering again. "This is no place for a woman."

"I can fend for myself."

"I am quite aware of that."

Was he thinking back to the day I'd captured him during his fishing expedition? I'd proven my capability then. And he'd seen me training at camp, had even sparred with me from time to time.

"I'd feel better if you were well away from here and safely back at camp."

"I am not going back." We'd argued about my presence in the expedition since leaving camp, and I refused to heed his admonition.

He shook his head, his hair gleaming like gold in the afternoon sunlight and his eyes reflecting the light-blue sky overhead. Though his hair and eyes were fair and beautiful, his features were hardened into granite, his knife in one hand and his spear in the other. The layer of scruff on his chin and jaw had grown thick but only made him all the more handsome.

His appearance was something I couldn't keep from noticing, especially because Irontooth had commanded us to spend every waking and sleeping hour together over the past fortnight since our wedding.

Though I tried not to look at or think about Mikkel, he was undeniably attractive and drew my attention regardless. I loathed myself for my weakness, particularly those times when he caught me staring. Like now.

As if he'd felt my examination, he slanted a sideways glance at me.

I shot my attention to the gully below. "The exchange of prisoners is always tense."

"It doesn't have to be."

"They will not understand why we are only returning Fowler and why you and Gregor are staying with us."

"I'll go down and explain it myself."

"If you get anywhere near them, they may take you back regardless of your wishes." Or maybe he would run at the chance to rejoin the other group and escape this marriage that had been foisted upon him.

He hadn't complained about our arrangement, had in fact appeared to be making the best of the situation. And that made me feel worse for using him and our marriage as a way to save Ruby. Especially because he'd gone out of his way to treat me politely, giving me plenty of privacy whenever I needed it, deferring to me on most decisions, and remaining chaste in every sense of the word.

We'd spent long hours fishing and hunting, collecting firewood and root vegetables, and joining in the weapons training Irontooth led every day. And though we hadn't recaptured the camaraderie of that first week when he was in the dungeon, we'd still had plenty of time to talk and get to know each other.

He'd told me more about his Testing, where his brothers had gone for their Testing, and how he hadn't been in communication with either of them since they left Scania in May. Vilmar had been relegated to laboring in the gem mines as a slave, and Kresten was a woodcutter in Inglewood Forest. He'd spoken of both men with the utmost respect.

In turn, I'd shared more about my family, mostly my love for my father and sister. And while he'd known a little bit about the history of the Great Isle, I'd told him more about my mother and her twin sister, Leandra, how their father, King Alfred the Peacemaker, had given each of them an inheritance. My mother's had been Warwick and the coveted white stone, believed to be the primary means of alchemy.

Mikkel had been curious about the white stone and alchemy, but I didn't want to talk about it for long. My mother had obsessed over the alchemy process while I was growing up, had spent countless hours and resources trying to unlock the secret ingredients so she could be the first to transform stones into gold. She loved her alchemy more than anything or anyone, including her family. And because of that, I resented everything having to do with it.

While Mikkel hadn't requested to see my face, he had asked me again to tell him what had happened to cause my blemish. I suspected he believed I was unbearably deformed and had no wish to see me for fear of knowing exactly the kind of woman he'd married. Thus, I told him I didn't want to speak about it and not to bring it up again.

I focused on a goshawk floating above the dark Scots pine trees. It was too distant to see its red eyes and white eyebrows, but the bird of prey, with its oddly colored eyes, somehow seemed to belong to the island.

Belong. The word opened up the wound in my heart, which I'd tried so hard to ignore these many months. I didn't belong anywhere—not in Warwick, not here on the island, and not even in Scania with Mikkel.

Though Mikkel had reassured me he intended to keep our marriage vows, I wouldn't hold him to his promise. As soon as I was settled in Scania with Ruby, I would proceed with an annulment nonetheless. Then he wouldn't be stuck with a wife he hadn't wanted, and he'd be free to marry the princess his advisors had arranged for him.

I scanned the gorge again for a sign of the warring tribe but glimpsed only the others of our party hidden in their strategic locations. "Perhaps your wish is to return to Blade's tribe."

"My wish is to solve the differences between the two groups peacefully, like adults, rather than fighting like barbaric children."

"Then you would return to Blade if given the chance?" I didn't know why I was baiting him, but suddenly I very much needed to know whether he wanted to stay with me of his own will or whether he'd rather leave. "If you would like to go, I shall not stop you."

I watched the goshawk circle and then swoop toward the river. Mikkel didn't speak, and I felt foolish for going on about whether he wanted to stay or not. Of course none of this was his desire. The primary thing holding him to the island was his Testing. He'd shown that he'd do anything to prove his worthiness to become the next king. If not for the Testing, he would have left me and the island behind long ago.

"Pearl," he said softly.

I shot him a cautionary look only to find his summer-blue eyes holding me captive.

"You agreed to call me Veil in public."

"We're alone."

He was right. Our spot behind a boulder above the river was secluded and private, except for Gregor, who had perched behind a boulder a dozen paces away. But like Mikkel, I'd grown accustomed to the servant's constant presence and hardly noticed him hovering anymore.

"No one will be the wiser if you slip away now." I gave him one last chance to leave.

"Pearl." His voice was so gentle it silenced me.

Embarrassed, I wanted to look away, but his kind

eyes still held mine.

"I am not leaving. Put it from your mind."

"'Tis my fault you are here and bound to me. If I had refrained from capturing you that day . . ."

"Then one of Irontooth's other pawns would have captured me instead."

"Pawns? Are you saying I am one of Irontooth's pawns?"

He returned his sharp gaze to the scenery. "You know that you are. He's your puppet master."

I nearly laughed at his analogy but caught myself. Instead, I shoved his arm. As he was balanced on the balls of his feet, the move threw him off-kilter. He grabbed at me to steady himself. In the process, however, he tipped sideways, landed on his back, and somehow pulled me down on top of him.

Letting my weapons fall idle, I sprawled across him, feeling the solidness of his chest keenly against mine along with the rise and fall of his breathing. "Take it back," I said, trying to salvage my dignity.

"Take what back?" His eyes took on a sparkle.

"That Irontooth is my puppet master."

"He is."

"No, he is not. Now retract your words, or I shall make you pay for them."

"How will you make me pay, my lady?" His lips quirked with the beginning of a smile.

The air around me felt suddenly lighter, headier. And for the first time in a long time—perhaps since my father died—something akin to happiness stole into the dark and lonely corridors of my heart.

"I shall think of something terrible."

"How terrible?"

I searched my mind for a retort but could find nothing fitting. "Terribly terrible."

One of his brows curved, and his smile broke free. The sight of it took my breath away. His smiles were rare, but they always transformed his face, taking away the cold sternness and replacing it with warm acceptance. It was the kind of expression that told me a future with this man would be graced with more smiles, laughter, and tenderness.

"I shall look forward to such *terribly terrible* consequences." His voice was light and teasing.

A lock of his fair hair had fallen across his forehead, and I reached up and smoothed it back, taking my time to tuck it into place.

As my fingers lingered in his hair, his breathing stilled and his smile faded.

Was he repulsed by my touch? I let my fingers fall away, self-conscious at my forwardness. But before I could get far, he snatched my hand and brought it to his lips. A soft, feathery warmth brushed my knuckles, and I sucked in a breath at the contact.

I didn't dare move for fear the moment might end before I was ready for it to.

Beneath me, his body remained motionless, and his eyes darkened to the color of the sky at twilight.

My heart began a strange thrumming of anticipation.

Ever so gently, he turned my hand over and pressed it against his lips, this time kissing the tender spot at the center of my palm.

His gaze held mine, unrelenting but tender, rendering me helpless and filling me with feelings for him I couldn't explain.

He lifted my hand away and curled my fingers closed, as if to keep his kiss there. At that instant, shouts from across the gorge jolted us. We scrambled to our knees and peered out, the intimacy dissipating under the harsh reality of where we were and the life we were leading.

At another shout, this one from the northern trail that wound up the island back to our camp, I spotted Tommy's bearlike frame. He limped forward, blood running down his face and disappearing into the thick hairy growth on his chin and neck. His eyes were wild and desperate, and he shouted again, this time more audibly. "The camp's been attacked!"

All around the gorge, our people tentatively stepped out of their hiding places, their faces confused. Irontooth emerged from his secluded spot closest to the river, Fowler bound and gagged beside him, along with several other of our fiercest warriors.

Mikkel's fingers tightened against both his weapons, as if he expected Blade's men to swoop out of the woods now that we'd revealed our positions.

"The camp!" Tommy fell to his knees, revealing a knife blade stuck deep into the flesh of his back.

I gasped and spun, ready to retrace my path along the cliff so I could race to his aid. Before I could take a step, Mikkel gripped my arm and stopped me. "Wait." He narrowed his eyes and scanned the landscape.

Irontooth had left Tommy back at our camp as he usually did to act as a sentinel and protect our position and few possessions. Had Blade lured us away from our camp on the pretense of the prisoner exchange only to attack while we were gone? That would explain why our rival and his men hadn't arrived yet at our prearranged meeting spot.

Tommy struggled to pick himself up. With his extraordinary strength, he somehow managed to stand and push farther toward the gorge. At the same time, several others from our group reached him and grabbed his arms, lending their support.

"What happened?" Irontooth shouted up at him, shielding his eyes with his hand against the bright summer sun. "Did Blade attack?"

Tommy shook his head, his expression radiating with both pain and devastation. "The Inquisitor, and his men! They took the women as prisoners and left me for dead."

The Inquisitor?

"Felicity?" Irontooth asked.

"Aye, she's gone." Tommy's voice cracked.

Irontooth dropped his hand from his eyes to his belt where he unsheathed his knife. With a roar that echoed all through the narrow valley, he bolted forward, racing up the trail that led back to camp.

The Inquisitor had Felicity and the two other women? My heart thundered with both pity and fear. How had this happened? Had Blade informed the Inquisitor we'd be away from camp, giving him the perfect opportunity to strike?

I jerked to free myself from Mikkel's grasp, but his fingers tightened around my arm.

"Release me."

"You're staying with me." His handsome features had turned to steel and his eyes to ice.

"I must go to Tommy. He needs my assistance, or he shall surely die."

Mikkel didn't loosen his grip. "I'll go with you."

I attempted to shrug off his hold again. "I do not

need you following my every move and acting as my bodyguard."

"You're my wife. I am duty bound to protect you."

I spun to face him. "I do not want your duty."

"You have it regardless." Any trace of the tender young man from moments ago was gone, and the regal prince with his lofty ideals was back in place. He'd been born and raised to be a prince and a king. He took his duties and vows seriously, and I could respect that.

But a small piece of my heart rebelled against his integrity and high standards. The part that longed for him to simply like me for who I was and not because he was bound to me.

His hard expression dared me to defy him again. I would have challenged him further if not for the urgency of Tommy's wound. "Very well," I whispered tersely. "Let us be on our way."

"Very well." His response was just as terse.

I glanced at his hand pointedly, and only then did he let go.

Chapter 11

MIKKEL

AT THE SIGHT OF THE DESTRUCTION WITHIN THE CAMP, I SANK TO the nearest boulder and shuddered. The caves had been emptied, and everything of value had been broken or burned.

The main thought reverberating through my mind was that if Pearl hadn't insisted on going to the prisoner exchange, the Inquisitor would have captured her along with Felicity and the other women.

"No sign of their boats," Toad called from the highest point of camp, a tall rock that gave a view of the northern side of the island and the sea surrounding it.

"They can't be far away." Irontooth didn't pause in strapping on his armor over his chain mail, armor now blackened from the Inquisitor's bonfire. "Everyone get ready to go! We'll leave right away and head after them."

"No." I pushed myself up. "You can't go yet."

"No one is asking for your opinion," Irontooth snapped.

I stalked toward him, my muscles tensing. This fearless

leader might intimidate everyone else into obeying him, but I refused to allow him to bully me. "You'll be a fool if you rush off after the Inquisitor."

"Stay out of this!" He glared at me—a look that said he wouldn't hesitate to beat me away if I dared try to stop him.

Pearl bolted up from where she was tending Tommy, and she took several rapid steps in my direction. Was she worried for me? Afraid of what Irontooth might do if I stood up to him?

I'd spent much time over the past couple of weeks studying the fearless leader and trying to see into his heart. And I'd come to understand that although Irontooth was a seasoned warrior and his tactics were sometimes unnecessarily brutal, he wasn't a killer.

I strode up to him and sent my fist flying into his face. At the crack of my knuckles against his cheek, pain radiated up my arm to my shoulder. But I unsheathed my spear and knife instantly, ready to fight.

Irontooth roared his anger and swung at me with his sword as I'd predicted.

Pearl shouted a warning, urging me to stop. But in all my recent analyzing, I'd surmised that the primary means of gaining his respect was by a show of force. He wouldn't listen any other way.

Of course, I had no aspirations to usurp his leadership. But I couldn't let him charge off in pursuit of the Inquisitor, not in his frenzied condition. Nothing good would come of leading with one's heart without also using one's head. And right now he was too upset at losing Felicity to think clearly.

He bellowed his pain and frustration, this time louder. Then he brought his sword down with an expertise and fortitude that gave me pause. This seasoned knight was a better fighter than I was. Had I jumped into the fray too quickly?

Even as doubts crowded in, I shoved them aside and forced myself to concentrate. In the wake of Irontooth's loss of the woman he loved, he was weak and vulnerable, and I would bring him to his knees to show him so.

I dodged several blows and warded off more with my spear. I could sense his vexation growing the longer I evaded him. And I toyed with him a moment longer, praying he would make a mistake before I did.

When he raised his sword above his head and lunged toward me, his momentum was too swift and desperate. It was the crack I'd been waiting for. As he swung down, I sidestepped, spun, and thrust the hilt of my sword into his back. The pressure caused him to trip and sent him sprawling to the ground, his arms outstretched. His sword slipped from his grip and clattered out of his reach.

I wasted no time in hopping onto his back and pressing my boot heel into the sensitive spot between his shoulder blades, also brushing the tip of my spear against the nape of his neck. He struggled until the blade pierced his skin and drew blood.

Even then, I remained alert. The moment I let down my guard, he'd buck me off and begin fighting again. I needed to speak reason into him now before he plotted his next move. Or before one of his men attacked me.

Already, several of the outcasts were closing in, weapons drawn, ready to bring me down.

"No doubt the Inquisitor and his men have hidden along the coast somewhere." I spoke loudly enough for everyone to hear. "They are hoping to draw us out by baiting us with the captives. If we leave now, we'll fall prey to their trap and deliver more of our group into their hands."

The men nearing me stopped, obviously heeding the truth of my words. I prayed Irontooth would as well.

"As hard as it may be, we must wait to go after the women."

"That's easy for you to say when your woman is safe." Bitterness edged Irontooth's voice, though he made no move to oust me.

Pearl had stopped a short distance away. Her weapons were drawn, and her brow creased. I wasn't sure if she'd intended to join the others in trying to stop my battle with the fearless leader or if she planned to come to my defense. Either way, her eyes radiated worry.

"I don't begrudge you your concern." I hastened to reason with Irontooth. "If our roles had been reversed, no doubt I would have insisted upon leaving forthwith. But I also know you would have stopped me from acting impulsively and forced me to see reason. And later, I would have thanked you for it."

Silence descended. Only the crackling of the bonfire filled the air.

"As it is," I continued, "we must not allow the Inquisitor to fool us again. Instead, we must fool him and devise a strategy not only to rescue the women but also to put an end to his terror once and for all."

"Hear, hear!" came the calls of some of the men.

Beneath me, I felt the fight begin to drain from Irontooth. Still, I didn't relent and kept my boot and spear taut and ready to fight this man again if need be.

"What strategy do you propose?" someone asked.

"We wait." I forced myself to think quickly. "And we attack when they're least expecting it."

More murmurs and calls of agreement confirmed I was accomplishing what I'd set out to do. After several more seconds, I released the pressure against Irontooth and took a step back. As he pushed himself off the ground, I didn't put my weapons away and prayed I wouldn't have to repeat the attack. The next time, without the element of surprise, I might not come out on top.

When Irontooth was on his feet again, he crossed his arms and glared at me.

I stared back, unyielding. I sensed he desperately wanted to leave to go after Felicity but that he also cared too much about the rest of his people to willingly put them in danger.

A trickle of blood ran from his nose down into his silver mustache and onto his lips. "Clean up the camp." He swiped at the blood. "Then we'll gather for a meeting to plan our attack."

He turned and stalked off toward his cave. The pain of his heartache radiated with each stride. But as difficult as losing Felicity was, Irontooth would do her no good if he were captured.

Sensing a presence by my side, I found Pearl next to me, staring sadly after Irontooth.

"He loves her, though he cannot admit it," she said.

"If he loves her, then he must think rationally before acting."

"Perhaps true love makes one do things one would not normally consider."

I didn't know. I'd never been in love. But I had been shaken by how close Pearl had come to being in captivity with the women. I might not love her the way Irontooth loved Felicity, but after all the time we'd spent together, I'd grown to care about her enough that I could empathize with Irontooth. Even if she was frustratingly stubborn at times . . .

She shifted her gaze to mine, the green turning as light as a summer meadow. My thoughts returned to the moment when she'd fallen on me, the way her touch in my hair ignited something inside me, and how soft her palm felt against my lips.

I'd never given attraction much consideration. As I'd told Pearl when I'd been locked up in the dungeon, I always believed that my marriage would be practical and necessary, and always considered love something one chose to give regardless of feelings.

But was it possible I might be developing an attraction to Pearl after all? And yet, how could I find a woman with blemishes appealing? Surely once I saw her full face without her veil, this draw to her would diminish.

I shook my head to clear it of the confusion. The truth was, the more I got to know Pearl, the more I liked who she was regardless of how she looked. She was a smart, vibrant, and interesting woman. Not only that, but she cared deeply about people, was sacrificial, and was willing to do hard things. And maybe all those qualities made her appear more attractive to me. Whatever the case, as she peered up at me, I lost myself in her beautiful eyes once again.

Was she looking at me with admiration? Or interest? Or even longing?

Surely not.

"You did the right thing even though it was hard."

Her praise warmed me every bit as much as her gaze. When she reached out and squeezed my arm, I suddenly felt as though I'd won the kingship.

"I should go to him." She glanced toward Irontooth's

cave. "I shall offer to take a group over to Fife under cover of darkness to trail the Inquisitor and—"

"No." The word was out before I could think, breaking me free from my trance. "I'll do it."

"I have lived here longer and know the patterns of the sea and Loch Ness better."

"It doesn't matter. I don't want you getting anywhere near the Inquisitor."

A crease formed between her brows, and her eyes sparked with the same fire I'd seen there many times since meeting her. "I am ready for something like this. 'Tis what I have trained for these many months."

"Now that we are married, you have no need of training or fighting." I hadn't spoken against her joining in the weapons drills in camp, primarily because she was safer if she could defend herself. But there was no good reason for her to participate in the conflict with the Inquisitor.

As though sensing my resolve to stop her, she took a step away. "So long as there are people in this world like Queen Margery, I shall always have need of training and fighting."

I wanted to contradict her, even forbid her from speaking to Irontooth. But at the glimpse of pain in her eyes, I held back my refusal. She was still working through a testing—a challenge—of her own. And she needed to resolve this inner battle if she would ever have true peace. But could I allow her to go on so perilous a mission?

I tried to gentle my tone. "'Tis my own fear of what may happen to you that makes me cautious."

"Then you think I am weak and incapable?"

"Not at all. You are one of the most capable ladies I have ever met."

"Then what?"

I glanced around to see who was observing our conversation. Only Gregor paid us any heed from where he stood next to our cave entrance. I rapidly closed the distance between Pearl and myself and took hold of both her arms.

She stiffened and struggled to pull away.

I slid my arms around her and pulled her into an embrace. I didn't have the words to express my feelings for her, not when I didn't fully understand them.

As our bodies made contact, she stilled.

I ran my hand down the long length of her braid and had the sudden vision of unraveling it and letting my fingers tangle in the ebony waves. I'd never seen her with her hair unbound but could imagine just how beautiful it would look.

She held herself rigidly a moment longer before she leaned in and rested her head against my chest. She didn't embrace me in return, but I prayed she understood that I cared about her and wished no harm to befall her.

As I released her and strode away, I could feel her gaze following me. I'd learned long ago that doing the unexpected was one easy way to disarm a person and defuse a tense situation. And now I wanted to turn around and gauge her expression, to look into her eyes and see if she was beginning to care about me—even if just a little.

But I forced myself to keep walking. Sometimes a person didn't recognize the value of what they had until it was no longer within reach.

Chapter
12

Pearl

The oars dipped in and out of the water, hardly making a sound.

My heartbeat made up for the silence and gonged as loudly as St. Matthew's Cathedral bell now ringing for Lauds. The majestic stone church stood at the center of Fife, one of Norland's southern ports and the city closest to our island. The echo of the early prayer hour reverberated in the darkness of predawn.

Kneeling in the middle of the boat, I focused on the water, keeping watch for any signs of Loch Ness. Beside me, Mikkel had taken the lookout on the other side. His attention hadn't strayed from the sea since we'd begun the crossing.

We hoped the Inquisitor wouldn't expect us at all during the night, since so few dared to traverse the sea while Loch Ness hunted. But if the Inquisitor had posted sentries, he would most likely place them at the easier, shallower crossings and not at the deepest section in the Channel, where sightings of Loch Ness along with strange drownings and disappearances were most frequent.

Loaded with six of us, the boat sat low, requiring those at the oars to press deeper, quite possibly drawing Loch Ness's attention. With the city looming ahead in the faint moonlight, I could only pray we'd bypassed the sea creature, but I wouldn't rest until I stood on land.

As it was, I squinted, looking for the telltale signs of bubbles and fish remains along with any unusual disturbances in the water.

"Halt!" Mikkel ordered in an urgent whisper.

The rowers stopped and lifted their dripping oars, resting them inside the boat. We waited silently, not daring to move, not even to swat at the mosquitoes and gnats buzzing around us.

With his spear drawn and poised above the lapping waves, Mikkel seemed to follow a trail. I couldn't see anything unusual, but his focus remained unswerving upon something below the surface.

Though his countenance was shadowed by the night, the outline of his face showed regal determination. From the way he held himself to the way he spoke, he commanded attention. Although the others now knew he was nobility, did any of them suspect his royalty? Every time I watched him, like when he'd fought Irontooth earlier, I waited for someone to point out that he behaved like a prince—or a king.

In truth, Mikkel had the makings of a great king. He was a natural leader with both wisdom and diplomacy, and yet he had shown incredible restraint in continuing to submit to Irontooth's direction. Even after subduing our fearless leader, Mikkel had walked away and resumed his position as a follower, allowing Irontooth to regain his dignity.

Rather than displaying irritation or dislike, Irontooth had tolerated Mikkel better than I'd expected. Perhaps because Mikkel would eventually leave, Irontooth realized the young prince was truly no threat. Or perhaps the incident today had given Irontooth more respect for Mikkel.

Whatever the case, from the bow, Irontooth watched Mikkel as though waiting for his cue on how to proceed, not the least perturbed Mikkel stood over him and had issued an order. Irontooth wouldn't have allowed anyone else to do so, not even me.

Perhaps his view of Mikkel had altered once he learned of his royalty. Of course, I didn't see Mikkel differently because he was a prince. I'd admired him since I first met him, and that hadn't changed ... except maybe I liked him more.

I couldn't stop thinking about the hug he'd given me at camp. I'd allowed my ire to get the better of me, snapping when he'd protested my involvement in tonight's expedition. Instead of demanding his way and engaging in a terse exchange, he'd wrapped me in his arms, touched my hair, and assured me his concern was genuine—all without words.

I was beginning to think I liked him too much and that I wouldn't be able to give him the annulment when the time came to do so.

Slowly, he pulled his arm back and tilted his spear down. At a ripple a dozen paces from the boat, I froze. From the many months of fishing around the island, I was familiar enough with the wave patterns, and what I'd just seen wasn't normal. It was likely the movement from where Loch Ness was circling our boat, trying to determine what we were and how she could best attack.

I shivered and followed the next ripple.

Though many had tried to kill the ancient sea creature over the decades, even centuries, no one had ever gotten close enough to destroy it before it rose from the water to strike.

Carefully, I readied my bow and arrow along with my knife. I could see the others preparing for an attack too. I could only pray Loch Ness didn't upend the boat. It was one of our bigger vessels and heavy under our weight. Nevertheless, Loch Ness was unpredictable, more so in recent months.

The ripple moved away and then circled back.

Mikkel lifted his spear higher. At his bravery in the face of this danger, I took a deep breath, prepared to fight this sea monster with the same courage.

Wordlessly we waited, and from the expressions on everyone's faces, I sensed they were drawing courage from Mikkel too. When, a moment later, a long tail humped above the surface and its scales glittered a silvery green in the moonlight, I notched my arrow, ready to let it fly.

Mikkel held out a hand to stop us from firing. After another long minute of the creature circling, the swell disappeared. Mikkel motioned for us to remain silent and still, and for endless seconds we sat without moving, the low waves bumping the hull.

"It's gone." Mikkel lowered himself to his knees. "Let us be on our way with all haste before it detects us again."

Immediately, the others slipped their oars into the

sea and rowed.

"Faster," Mikkel urged.

The boat moved forward at a swift speed, the men hurrying to obey Mikkel. I wished I could lend them my aid, but I continued to survey the sea the same as Mikkel, praying we would be able to outpace Loch Ness.

As we drew nearer to the shore, the fear of Loch Ness meshed with a fear of the Inquisitor's retinue of soldiers, enlisted to aid him in his efforts to purify the Church and the land of infidels. We would need to use extreme caution as we navigated the streets and alleys of the city in an effort to discover where the Inquisitor was holding the women.

During our meeting at camp earlier, we'd discussed all the options and come up with several likely places. We'd decided to split up so we could stay hidden better. One pair would search St. Matthew's Cathedral. Another would investigate the local lockup. And Mikkel and I planned to head to the town market and public green. Mikkel had insisted on being with me, although Gregor wanted to come too and had reluctantly conceded to being with one of the other outcasts.

We directed the boat toward a wharf on the far end of town where the buildings were older and the shacks run-down. A few upstairs windows reflected low candlelight, but otherwise, the town was asleep.

When the boat thumped against the pier, Mikkel was the first to leap out, then reached back in to assist me. In my usual hose and breeches, I'd donned a cloak to hide my long hair and prevent anyone from seeing me. Though the summer nights in Norland were cooler than Warwick's, the cloak was heavy and oppressive in the humidity that hung in the air.

Mikkel leaned in, his face nearly touching mine. "Ready?"

I nodded. Already the other outcasts were slinking away in pairs, disappearing into the shadows.

"Stay right behind me," he whispered.

"I shall lead," I whispered back. "I know the way better."

He shook his head, his nose brushing my cheek. "Irontooth explained where we need to go, and I shall lead."

I started to shake my head, but he pressed in closer so his lips almost touched my ear, distracting me and silencing me at the same time.

"I conceded in letting you come." His whisper turned harsh. "Don't make me regret it."

Before I could protest any further, he started toward the nearest building, racing fast but crouching low. We flew down one dark street after another, keeping to the back ways and ducking into alleys the instant we heard any noise but our own.

As we reached the town green, we cautiously peeked out of an alley. Immediately, Mikkel ducked back and pushed me behind him.

"What—?" I started to whisper only to have him clamp a hand over my veil and mouth.

He spun me around so my back was against the cool wattle-and-daub exterior of the closest business. And then he startled me by practically throwing himself against me.

"A soldier," he whispered against my ear. "Pretend to be kissing me."

"But my veil—"

"Pull it down." He glanced over his shoulder, his voice urgent and his body stiff.

I hesitantly tugged.

"Hurry." He pushed off my hood and let my long hair show before bracing his elbows on either side of my face. He leaned his face in so our noses touched but the veil still covered my mouth.

I loosened the ribbons that held it firmly in place and lowered it farther so my mouth was free. With the darkness of the alley along with his shadow falling over me, I doubted he could see anything except my outline. Even so, I trembled at the prospect of him seeing me—truly seeing me—for the first time.

At the slap of nearing footsteps, I brushed my nose against his. I'd never kissed a man, much less pretended to do so, and I was at a loss for how to proceed. "How shall I pretend—?"

His mouth captured mine, cutting off my words. Warmth and power and passion pulsed against me, and suddenly I was lost in the connection, lost in a beautiful place I'd never gone before.

Vaguely, I could hear the thud of steps turning into the alley, but I was too enamored by the feel of Mikkel's lips upon mine and somehow needed to respond. In fact, his kiss seemed to demand something from me in return. I could do nothing less than move my lips with his.

"What's going on?" said a gruff voice from a few paces away.

Mikkel abruptly ended the kiss but continued to recline against me, his elbows resting nonchalantly against the wall though his muscles tensed. "I think it's obvious what's going on, don't you?" He attempted a note of humor before he leaned in, touching his lips to mine once more.

Although Mikkel was pretending at kissing me, the sensation was unlike anything I'd ever known, and I didn't need to feign an interest in reciprocating. I rose up again, this time eagerly. And I pressed into him more thoroughly, kissing him back with as much fervor as he'd kissed me.

"Take it inside." The soldier's gruff voice was also laced with mirth.

"Excellent idea." Mikkel broke away for an instant before I chased his lips and found them, giving him no choice but to kiss me again.

The soldier snorted a laugh before he moved out of the alley, his footsteps retreating to wherever he'd been before we'd made him aware of our presence.

I didn't care about the soldier, didn't care about our rescue mission, didn't care about the peril hovering around every corner. All I could think about was Mikkel kissing me and that I didn't want him to stop.

His lips and his touch had unearthed in me a wellspring of emotions I couldn't begin to name, so when he broke the kiss, I clutched his tunic and held him in place. My movement must have given him some kind of permission to continue, because he seized my mouth again with a fervor that sent tingles over my skin and down my backbone.

As though forcing himself, he broke away and leaned his head against the wall so our cheeks brushed. "We have to go," he whispered breathlessly. "Before he comes back and asks more questions."

I nodded, too overwhelmed to say anything. Who

could have guessed that kissing Mikkel would be like this? My legs shook beneath me, hardly able to hold me up. And as I released his garment, my fingers trembled.

In spite of his admonition to be on our way, he didn't make an effort to move. Instead, his presence surrounded me. His scruffy cheek pressed to mine, and his ragged breathing filled my ear, sending more tremors through me.

"Pearl." His voice filled with something I could only describe as wanting. Was it possible these kisses hadn't been pretend for him either? Was it possible he was feeling the same desire for me that I was for him?

My heartbeat tapped out an uncertain rhythm. What did this mean for our relationship? And where did we go from here?

"Pearl." This time he pulled slightly away. "You must—you need to—"

I waited for him to tell me what to do next. He obviously had more practice at relationships than I did and would know how to proceed.

"You have to put your veil back on," he finished.

I stiffened. "Why?"

"It's just better that way."

Better for whom? For him? So he didn't have to chance seeing my so-called blemish? I pushed him away and, at the same time, tugged up the veil.

"Don't be upset," he whispered. "If the guards see your flaws, they'll know who we are and that we've come for the women."

"Or maybe you have no wish to see who I really am because you fear you will not like how I look." The hurt welling up inside pushed me to taunt and test him. Was he so shallow he couldn't abide seeing my face? If that was the case, I would keep myself hidden from him.

"That's not it." But the hint of uncertainty in his voice told me he was indeed afraid of finally seeing the real woman he'd married.

I shoved his chest, forcing him to take a step back. Then I turned away from him as I tied the veil into place.

Behind me, he released an exasperated breath. "I'm sorry. I shouldn't have allowed us to get so carried away—"

"I was only pretending, as you asked of me." I spun around and glared at him, his rejection stinging. "You need not flatter yourself into thinking I liked kissing you." I had more than liked it. I'd adored it. But I couldn't allow him to think so and pity me.

Any response he might have had ready, he let fade to silence.

I cinched the veil strings, putting the barrier back between us where it belonged. Disappointment wedged there too. Always before, I'd had to wonder if the men at court could see beyond my beauty and royalty and appreciate my other qualities. And now I faced the same problem, only slightly different. Could men—particularly Mikkel—see beyond my veil and perceived ugliness to like me for who I was on the inside?

The truth was, I didn't want to be loved for what I looked like for either the good or the bad. I wanted to be loved for who I was. Was that too much to ask?

Chapter 13

MIKKEL

I TURNED AWAY FROM PEARL TO ALLOW HER TO FINISH TYING HER veil into place. All the while, my pulse slammed hard through my veins with a sizzling heat.

What had just happened between us?

At the sight of the guard, I'd panicked and taken the first excuse that came to mind—the only one I could think of for why a man and woman would be out so early in the morn together: that we were helplessly in love with each other.

I'd thought pretending at kissing would prove our ruse. But all it proved was how little self-control I had.

I pressed my palm against my forehead and closed my eyes, attempting to slow my racing thoughts even if I couldn't slow my pulse. But my mind had a will of its own and relived the kisses again, especially the taut grip of her fingers against my tunic as she'd held me—almost as if she'd wanted me in that moment as much as I had her.

Almost.

I'd endeavored to pretend, but the moment my mouth

had met hers, I'd lost all reason. It had been an explosive union, one that had set me on fire and nearly made me forget where we were and the danger lurking so near.

"'Tis back in place," she whispered. "You need not worry that I shall scare you."

"I wasn't worried about that." Frustration coursed through me, aimed more at myself than at her. For amidst her accusation, I feared a hint of truth lingered, that I was placing too much emphasis on her appearance. Had I been doing so with all the outcasts?

Look on the heart. I'd believed the purpose of my Testing was to analyze the behaviors and motivations of the people I met. And maybe that was part of it. But perhaps I needed to reevaluate what I was doing, see beyond the exterior and evaluate the worth of a person's character more than anything else.

Could I do that with Pearl? Place more importance on her character than her blemish?

I swiveled back to her. She was halfway down the alley, racing back the way we'd come. "Wait."

She didn't halt or even slow down. Instead she reached the end building, hopped up onto a barrel, leapt for the projecting beam of the second floor, and then hefted herself up until she gripped a windowsill. Before I could make it to the barrel, she was already standing on the sill and reaching for the overhanging roof. She grabbed on to one of the rafters and swung herself until she looped a leg onto the slate tiles.

She made the climb look so effortless, and perhaps it was for a nimble woman of her size. However, I struggled to follow the trail she'd made. By the time I reached the roof, she was lying on her stomach, peering over the top to the other side of the businesses.

"What do you see?" I whispered, as I crawled up next to her as quietly as I could manage. The last thing we needed was for anyone sleeping in the dormer room below us to hear our pattering around and come outside to investigate.

"The women are here." Her response was quiet, resigned.

I lifted my head cautiously so I could see over to the town green.

"They are bound in the stocks."

The moonlight illuminated the open area enough to see three planks, bare feet and ankles poking through the crude holes, locking the women in place. Though the stocks rested on the ground and allowed the women to sit with their legs outstretched, the angle was such that no amount of shifting in position would allow even an ounce of comfort.

With heads bowed and shoulders slumped, the three appeared to be resting to some degree. And from what I could assess, they hadn't been harmed, at least not severely.

Felicity's white hair was the most obvious, in the middle. One of the other women, who went by the nickname Rose, had a rose-colored splotch on half her face. The older woman everyone called Joan was deaf and mute. The three spent most of their time preparing meals and keeping the camp in order, unlike Pearl, who went everywhere with the men.

"I see half a dozen of the Inquisitor's guards." Pearl leaned in, her face near mine. "One on nearly every corner."

I counted the well-armed guards, including the one who had witnessed our kisses. "The Inquisitor has placed the women in the town green specifically to draw us out into the open to trap us. We won't be able to get near the women, not without eliciting the attention of the guards."

Pearl ducked her head down. "Then we shall have to fight them in order to free the women. With only six of them to our six, the clash should be evenly matched."

I shifted out of sight as well. "No doubt these soldiers are seasoned, skillful, and have superior weapons. We would have a difficult fight ahead."

"I am ready for the challenge."

"Rushing out there would bring death to us all."

"You have no faith in our abilities?"

"I have every faith the Inquisitor has more soldiers nearby who would join their comrades at a moment's notice, quickly outnumbering us."

Lying flat and propped up by her elbows, she was a hand's span away, staring straight ahead at the roof tiles, her forehead wrinkled. "What shall we do?"

"We shall meet Irontooth and the others at the arranged spot and then come up with a plan." Still, I sensed the futility of the mission. How would we liberate the women without putting everyone else in jeopardy?

"You do not believe we can rescue them, do you?"

I hesitated. I believed in honesty, even when the truth was difficult to abide. But I wanted to reassure Pearl everything would work out so she didn't charge forward recklessly and end up in the stocks next to the others.

She released a frustrated huff from behind her veil and started to slither backward.

I slipped an arm around her waist, halting her progress.

"Whether you realize it or not, you're the leader of this expedition." Her whisper was low and fierce. "And as the leader, if you have no hope, you will convey your hopelessness to the others. Then we shall surely fail."

Her words gave me pause. Somehow I had ended up the leader. As such, I needed to guide by example. "You're right. I must put aside my fears and find hope."

The tension eased from her body.

I tucked her head under my chin and closed my eyes. We lay side by side, neither of us speaking. "Thank you for saying what I needed to hear," I whispered. "And I am heartily sorry for my insensitivity regarding your veil after our kiss. I hurt you, and I regret it."

She nodded, making no move to pull away.

We rested that way for a few more moments before she leaned back enough that I could see her eyes. "In watching you these past weeks, I have seen that you will make a good and wise king. Your father and his advisors would be foolish not to choose you."

"Thank you, Pearl." I marveled at how she had a way of encouraging me like no one else had ever been able to do. A part of me wished we could go on lying on the roof whispering to each other. I liked spending time with her, especially moments like this when we understood each other.

But the night was slipping away, and we had a mission to accomplish. We needed to find a way to rescue the women from their stocks without anyone else getting captured or killed.

Wordlessly, I released her and began the climb back down. She followed, and though she didn't need my aid, I waited and assisted her as much as she would let me. When she finally stood next to me in the alley, I reached for her hand, wrapped my fingers around hers, then started to the ash pit on the outskirts of town where we'd arranged to meet the others.

She didn't release my hand, and somehow, even the small connection was all I could think about as we traveled. Next time we went somewhere, I needed to keep Gregor close by, since I was too distracted. And distraction could oft be dangerous.

As we neared the ash pit, the scent of garbage and waste grew so putrid I had to breathe through my mouth to keep from gagging. I understood now why Irontooth had arranged for our meeting in this location. It was deserted and the perfect place to avoid detection.

I tugged Pearl down behind a barrel overflowing with trash and searched for signs of the others. But everything was eerily silent and still.

Next to me, Pearl gasped and tugged her hand free of my grip. She groped after a sheet of parchment on the ground. When she picked it up, her fingers trembled.

"What is it?" I asked.

She handed it to me. There, in calligraphy, were the words: *"A large reward shall be given to the person who finds Princess Pearl of Warwick. Wanted for the high crime of treason."*

Even through the darkness of the early morning hour, the words were dark and bold. I lifted the parchment higher into the moonlight to read the smaller paragraph underneath.

"Her Royal Highness, Queen Margery of Warwick, has issued a reward to anyone who can deliver the princess to her alive. Once believed dead, the princess is known to have run away and is hereby charged with conspiracy along with her sister, Princess Ruby, in attempting to overthrow the throne."

Pearl's hand shook as she took the sheet away from

me and scanned it again. "My mother knows I am alive."

"You guessed that might be a possibility, did you not?"

"Yes, but why is she charging me with treason?"

The queen was clearly searching hard if she had notices posted all the way in Norland.

"Why now? After all this time?" Pearl's whisper was threaded with both fear and frustration. "And why is she involving Ruby?"

"Perhaps this notice is old."

Pearl pointed to a small set of numerals at the end. "'Twas penned right after Midsummer's Eve and likely sent out by couriers to the far corners of the Great Isle."

Midsummer's Eve was over a month ago. "Maybe she recently discovered you didn't die in the hunting accident."

"'Tis possible. But why threaten Ruby? She is too young and too innocent to be of use to the queen."

I could come up with only one reason why. "The logical explanation is that the queen intends to use your sister to lure you back to Warwick."

Pearl dropped the sheet and then bent over and buried her face in her hands. She released a soft groan that ended on a sob.

I placed a hand on her back, wanting to comfort her but unsure how. Ruby meant everything to her, was important enough that Pearl had agreed to marry me in order to save her sister and give her a new home.

Before I could figure out what to say, Pearl rose to her feet, her eyes flashing with determination. "I need to leave now and go after her."

She started to stalk away, but I lunged for her. Pearl couldn't just leave for Warwick. Such notices were likely posted in every town and hamlet from here to Warwick.

People would be eager to find the princess and turn her over to the queen so they could claim the reward.

Anyone could piece together the truth and betray her. Pearl wouldn't be safe anywhere. Not even on the Isle of Outcasts.

Even as she struggled against me, I pinned her arms to her side. After experiencing her fighting skills firsthand and watching her train, I anticipated her elbow jab and the ensuing flip. I blocked her and twisted her arm behind her back to subdue her. Of course, I didn't twist hard, just enough to keep her from moving.

"Release me at once," she hissed.

"You cannot run off by yourself," I whispered from behind her. "You will rush right into the queen's hands, which is exactly what she wants. And if she captures you, how will you rescue Ruby then?"

Pearl held herself rigid for another moment before she sagged into me. She pressed her hands against her veil and mouth but couldn't muffle her cry of despair. I cupped my hand over hers to aid in stifling the sound. I wrapped my other arm around her and leaned in so my mouth brushed against her ear. "Shh . . . we'll figure out what to do. I promise."

Even as I spoke, my mind scrambled to come up with a viable plan, one that would keep Pearl out of the queen's clutches. If the woman had attempted to kill her daughter once before, what was to keep her from trying again?

My gut churned at the prospect. I didn't want Pearl to get anywhere near Queen Margery. And yet, I couldn't stop her from helping Ruby. She'd go whether or not I wanted her to.

Ultimately, we needed to gain access to Ruby without putting either of us in jeopardy. Perhaps wielding my royalty as a weapon was the only way. I would have to go with Pearl and lend her my protection as her husband and as a prince of Scania.

But doing so would mean having to leave the Isle of Outcasts and my Testing. Could I really withdraw from the challenge and forfeit my chance at becoming king? After all, the reason I'd married Pearl was so I wouldn't have to stop and go home in disgrace.

Shaking my head with mounting frustration, I glanced around the ash pit as if I could somehow find the answers there. But the desolate place contained nothing but the rotting mounds of garbage along with the incinerating ovens and the ash heaps next to them.

Would my hopes and dreams turn to ashes? Or could I continue my Testing somehow? Was it possible that, if I left with Pearl and helped recover Ruby, I could return to the island afterward? The rules stated that if we princes needed to leave our locations for any reason, we could go back and finish to the best of our ability.

"I shall travel with you," I whispered. "And when we get there, I'll negotiate for Ruby's release."

"She will never hand Ruby over to you. Not if she wants me."

I recognized the truth in Pearl's words, which stirred my fear. "Then the question we must answer is, why does she want you back?"

"To attempt to kill me again?"

"But why did she try to kill you the first time? And why would she want to do so again?"

"She believes I am plotting treason, perhaps even amassing followers who will rise up and lead a revolt against her."

During one of our many conversations, we'd discussed

Warwick's increasing poverty as a result of the gemstone mine not producing as many precious jewels in recent years. And we'd also talked about the queen's yearly custom of sacrificing a maiden to a berserker—a madman—by the name of Grendel and how the people resented the choosing process. It was easy to see why the people might want to revolt.

Nevertheless, in all my analyzing, I still hadn't been able to understand why Queen Margery had tried to eliminate Pearl. Even if the queen despised Pearl's blemish or felt threatened by revolt, why not simply lock her up?

Plotting murder didn't make sense, and this charge of treason was even more far-fetched. The queen didn't truly believe her daughters, especially Ruby, who was just a child, could conspire against her. I could only puzzle over the queen's real motives for wanting Pearl to return.

A rat scurried past our feet, and Pearl hugged her arms over mine. "I shall not allow you to give up your Testing to accompany me. You must remain here—"

"And I shall not allow you to fight this battle against the queen alone."

"Mikkel, please. You must finish your Testing and become the great king you were destined to be."

I was grateful for her desire to see me succeed. But I could never count myself a great king if I consented to her wish to fend for herself while I pursued selfish gain. "Perhaps after we have Ruby, you can take her to Scania and wait for me there while I go back to the island and finish my Testing."

She hesitated. "This is too risky. I cannot ask this of you—"

"You're not asking." I tried to infuse my voice with princely authority so she would accept my decision. "I'm your husband now, and we shall face the queen together."

Two forms slinked into view a short distance away, Gregor and Irontooth. I grabbed the edict with the information about Pearl and crumpled it. I couldn't trust anyone else with keeping Pearl safe.

"Speak of this to no one," I whispered. "We shall finish our mission here in Fife. And once the women are safely returned to the island, we shall sneak away."

"Very well."

I released my hold of her, though I was loathe to do so. "Promise you will wait for me?"

She nodded almost imperceptibly.

Even with her reluctant vow, I feared I wouldn't be able to keep her safe, no matter how hard I tried.

Chapter 14

Pearl

I waited on the rooftop, where Mikkel had instructed me to stay. The setting sun on the horizon cast a blood-red glow over the town center, as if it had pronounced judgment and death upon the waiting women.

I shifted to get more comfortable, but the ache in my chest remained. It hadn't gone away since the moment I'd seen Ruby's name on the sheet of parchment hours ago. Every time I thought about what the queen was doing to my sister, the bitterness swelled until it nearly choked me.

My consolation was that my mother wouldn't try to murder Ruby, not as long as she needed my sister to draw me back to Warwick. At least I prayed so.

At the sight of a hooded man slipping through the gathering crowd, I rose to my knees, straightened my bow, and took out an arrow. On the rooftop adjacent to mine, Humphrey readied his bow and arrow too, his hood pulled up to cover his large head and ears.

The Inquisitor's soldiers had been laboring for the

past couple of hours at erecting stakes and piling wood around them. The women were still in the stocks where they'd languished all day in the unrelenting sun without food or water. The longer they suffered, the more anxious I was to relieve them.

But like everyone else, I respected Mikkel's plan and was following every detail. Once again, he'd shown himself to be a cunning and strategic leader. He'd solicited advice from the others and combined those suggestions into an ultimate rescue effort. Now, after the agonizing wait, we would soon set the plan into motion.

Since the Inquisitor still had lookouts posted along the harbor, we guessed he didn't yet realize we'd crossed over from the island. I prayed that meant our landing and positions hadn't yet been discovered.

Once we freed the women, we had a narrow window of time for making the escape, and we needed everything to go right. The trouble was that the slightest wrong move could jeopardize the under-taking, putting Mikkel in grave peril. And the thought of something happening to him added to the ache in my chest.

All day, as I'd stayed hidden on the roof, my mind had wandered to Mikkel. Even if he was still somewhat leery about what lay beneath my veil, he'd chosen—no, insisted—on going with me to rescue Ruby.

"I'm your husband now, and we shall face the queen together."

His passionate words reverberated through me again, as did the remembrance of the way he'd held my hand on the walk to the ash pit. Of course he'd been right to stop me from acting rashly after learning of

Ruby. And his comforting hold and his wise words had calmed me.

Through it all, I couldn't help liking him more and not less.

I watched him weave through the crowd, my chest squeezing with anxiety again. He'd insisted on being the one to make the public appearance, since no one would recognize him as an outcast. Hopefully, by the time the guards realized he was on our side, it would be too late. Irontooth stood on the outskirts along with Toad. With gloves covering his webbed fingers, Toad would blend in as well.

As Mikkel edged closer to the women, the Inquisitor stepped out of a nearby tavern. We'd guessed he would start the fires as soon as the sun set. He was giving us as much time as possible to make the crossing before nightfall. With the fear of being on the sea and encountering Loch Ness, he probably surmised that if we hadn't arrived by sunset, we weren't coming.

Little did he know that, since we'd crossed safely last night, we'd decided to chance the return trip in the dark as well. Our hope was that the Inquisitor and his men wouldn't try to follow us, would leave us to the fate of Loch Ness.

Attired in the long brown robes that priests wore, the Inquisitor was taller and thinner than most people, and his hair was shorn almost to his scalp, giving him a skeletal appearance.

From a distance, I'd once mistaken him for an outcast. He had an odd appearance, and most certainly could have fit into one of the island's groups. Because of that, his zeal for persecuting the misfits made little sense. I'd concluded that perhaps tyrannizing others made him feel better about himself.

He'd been hunting down and terrorizing the outcasts since before I'd arrived in the area. The last time two of our men had been captured, he hadn't waited to kill them. He'd taken them directly to the town square and riddled them with arrows.

Apparently today he was hoping to capture more outcasts. Maybe he was tired of the chase. Or maybe his superiors were pressuring him to increase his efforts. Regardless, we desperately needed to succeed this time and send him a message that he couldn't so easily intimidate us.

As the Inquisitor strode toward the town green, the villagers quieted and parted, making a path for him. Two armored guards followed on his heels, bringing the total soldiers up to ten—at least that I'd counted.

The odds weren't in our favor. But if we stayed focused and each did our part, Mikkel had assured us we would be fine.

I shifted my attention to his broad shoulders outlined beneath the cloak as he neared the stocks. He hadn't wanted me to participate in the rescue efforts, only reluctantly agreed to give me the rooftop spot. I'd been frustrated at his stubbornness. But now in watching him inch closer to danger, my stomach clenched. What if he'd simply been worried about what might happen to me the same way I was now with him?

When the Inquisitor reached the center, he proceeded toward the grouping of stakes and wood, walking around each one, picking up a piece of wood and pushing against the stakes. Then he took a spot nearby where he could see everything. He gave a nod to the soldiers guarding the women. They unlocked and lifted the top boards of the stocks so the prisoners could free their legs from confinement.

The women hurried to obey the command to stand. But because they'd been sitting for so long, they struggled to push themselves up, gaining kicks and rough prodding from the soldiers. The oldest of the three, Joan, fell to her knees every time she tried to rise, until Felicity stooped and slipped an arm around the woman's waist.

Now that the women were temporarily unbound, we needed to act. My attention shifted to Mikkel, and my muscles tensed. He'd already jumped up onto an overturned crate and tossed back his hood, revealing his handsome and yet commanding features. He stuck his fingers into his mouth and produced a piercing whistle that silenced the crowd and drew the gazes of everyone present.

Immediately, from opposite sides, Irontooth and Toad began to weave through the gathering toward the women.

"Citizens of Fife." Mikkel's voice rang out, the authority of his tone garnering even more attention so that no one paid Irontooth and Toad any heed. "What kind of city and nation have you become to sentence three women to death without the benefit of a fair trial?"

Murmurings arose from the crowd, and the Inquisitor's eyes widened as he took in Mikkel.

"If you judge by appearances alone and refuse to see deeper into the heart, you will only condemn yourselves to more judgment. Eventually, you will soon find yourselves standing in this very place, waiting to be burned at the stake. For who amongst us is without a flaw?"

The women had stopped the moment they heard Mikkel's voice, but thankfully Felicity was smart enough not to show her surprise. Instead, she kept her expression neutral and casually glanced over the crowd. I could tell the moment she glimpsed Irontooth by the way her back straightened.

I prayed strength would return to their limbs, allowing them to make their getaway quickly. Their lives would depend upon it.

"Who are we to say what is unnatural?" Mikkel continued, drawing the Inquisitor's scowl. "If you can revile one woman for a mark upon her face, then how could you not denounce another for a mark, only smaller? And if you condemn someone for pale skin and hair, then what's to stop you from casting judgment on a person with dark skin and hair?"

The Inquisitor motioned toward his guards, indicating they should silence Mikkel. But they were distracted by his speech. And they were also too distracted to see Irontooth and Toad drawing ever nearer to the women.

"How can we discount the value of this older woman who cannot speak, and yet nurture a wee babe who is guilty of the same?" Mikkel's impassioned pleas stirred the crowd, drawing choruses of agreement. "If we judge a person based solely on the way they stand apart from others, then why not judge the Inquisitor? He is taller and thinner than most."

At Mikkel's declaration, the Inquisitor's visage darkened, and he barked out more urgent orders to his guards, finally drawing their attention.

"Will you arrest me then also?" Mikkel was regal and every inch a prince. "Perhaps because I have blue eyes instead of brown?"

The agitation amongst the gathering was growing, just the way Mikkel had predicted it would. They began to jostle and push forward, which aided the momentum of Irontooth and Toad as they attempted to get next to the women.

"Rather than condemning some to be outcasts," Mikkel continued above the commotion, "let us recognize we are all unique and imperfect in some way. Let us find no shame in that and instead value each other for our differences."

With the Inquisitor's displeasure ringing in the air, the guards hastened toward Mikkel, though their steps were impeded by the surging crowd.

"Let the women go free!" Mikkel's cry rose strong and clear. "Do not make them suffer any longer for the superstitions of the Inquisitor."

I drew the bowstring taut. Mikkel had warned Humphrey and me not to shoot unless absolutely necessary. He hadn't wanted to draw attention to my position on the roof, which would make my getaway all the more difficult.

Even so, my muscles contracted with the need to protect Mikkel. If any of the soldiers threatened him, I doubted I'd be able to hold back, especially if he was in any danger of being captured.

Mikkel scanned the crowd. Seeing the guards fighting their way through the crowd in his direction, he hopped down from his perch, accepting the backslaps and arm squeezes of the people around him.

Already, Irontooth had reached Felicity and

scooped Joan up into his arms. Toad had a hold of Rose, and the group was making their escape.

Mikkel had instructed me to leave once we had possession of the women. Humphrey and I were to take back alleys and meet everyone at the boat. But I couldn't take my attention from Mikkel. Not yet. Not until I knew he was safe.

As the soldiers veered nearer to him, my pulse raced harder. I closed one of my eyes and sighted down the length of my arm and the arrow.

Just then, Mikkel spun and headed toward the Inquisitor.

"No," I whispered, silently urging him to flee the opposite way. But Mikkel managed to slip expertly through the crowd until he stood in front of the Inquisitor. He spoke something that caused the Inquisitor's face to deepen in color before he bellowed at his guards.

Mikkel picked up his pace, heading in the opposite direction from the rescue party. And suddenly I understood what he was doing. He was drawing the attention of the guards and the Inquisitor away from the others and placing it squarely upon himself.

As he disappeared between two buildings, my heart plummeted.

"Veil." A loud whisper came from the alley below me. "Come on. We have to go."

Humphrey was following Mikkel's instruction to get out of the area of the town square just as soon as we could before the Inquisitor realized the women were gone and called for reinforcements.

I strained to see Mikkel, but he'd disappeared, and now the soldiers were chasing after him. My heart thudded with fresh dread.

Even though I was tempted to rush to his aid, I resisted the impulse and did as Mikkel had wanted. I forced myself to climb down and slink away through the darkening shadows with Humphrey. Surely Mikkel would find a way to hide and outsmart the guards. If only I could convince my heart to believe my head.

By the time Humphrey and I reached the boat, the last rays of sunlight had faded, leaving darkness in its wake. I prayed the night would give the others an advantage, especially Mikkel as he ran for his life.

"We need to get out of sight." Humphrey settled low in the hull and motioned at me to do the same.

I hesitated, watching the shore. Lights flickered in the windows of some of the nearby buildings. Laughter and music seeped out the open doorway of what appeared to be a tavern. At least the people in this area of town were ignorant about the events at the town square. Or if they happened to know, they didn't seem to care.

With each passing minute, fear ticked louder within me. How could I hide away if Mikkel remained in peril? "Perhaps I shall make my way back to the north end and see if Mikkel needs my assistance."

"No." Humphrey's big eyes peered at me from the shadows of his hood. "You can't go. I promised Mikkel I'd make you stay."

I wanted to argue with Humphrey, but I liked knowing Mikkel had cared enough about me to plan for my safety. Only reluctantly did I flatten myself, and only because a group of revelers passed by. When a couple stumbled toward the wharf shortly after, I blew out a frustrated breath. Then I sat up as I recognized Toad and Joan.

Hurriedly, we assisted them into the boat and then remained motionless, praying no one had noticed us. After several minutes of silence, broken only by the sloshing of the waves against the boat and the voices from the nearby tavern, I poked my head up again to have Toad force it back down.

He was in the process of giving Joan a sip of water from his leather drinking pouch. And his efforts to bring the dear woman comfort put me to shame. I was more concerned about myself and Mikkel than about Joan and her suffering.

Thankfully, we didn't have to wait long for Irontooth and Felicity to appear with Rose. The women practically fell into the hull, breathing hard and shaking. I hugged them both, rejoicing in their safety, and then offered them the water and a slight bit of bread and dried fish that remained from the supplies we'd brought with us.

"Let's go," Irontooth said after he'd taken a long drink.

I glanced to the city, praying I'd see Mikkel creeping toward us, but none of the loiterers bore his strength or build. "We need to wait for Mikkel and Gregor."

Irontooth tugged at the stern line, his paddle in hand. "He told us if he wasn't here when we arrived, we needed to leave without him."

"No!" I dove forward. But I wasn't fast enough. He'd unhooked our connection to shore, and the boat began drifting away.

The other men had grabbled paddles and were digging into the water.

"We're not leaving without them." I lunged for Irontooth's oar, intending to wrest it from him.

He shifted it out of reach. "He told us to go because he knows we need to get away from here as soon as possible. If we don't go now, we might not make it across."

I held back my protest so that it burned in my throat. The longer we delayed our departure, the greater the chances of facing Loch Ness again. Or the Inquisitor. We'd made it this far with the women. We couldn't take any chances of the Inquisitor catching up to us now.

"He and Gregor can hide for the night," Irontooth said, "and then find a way back to the island tomorrow."

He was trying to reassure me, but my body tensed with increasing anxiety.

"He's an intelligent man." Irontooth lowered the paddle back into the water, steering the boat so the stern faced the open sea. "And he'll find a way to escape."

Felicity squeezed my shoulder. "He saved our lives. And if he ends up in danger because of it, we'll find a way to help him in return."

I nodded. Of course we would. But even as the words formed on the tip of my tongue, emotion flooded me so strongly I wanted to weep. I couldn't abide the thought of leaving Mikkel behind at the mercy of the Inquisitor. It was the same feeling I'd had when I left Ruby, but this was worse.

Shouts and the pounding of footsteps sounded from the wharf as two figures emerged from the darkness. At a distance of at least a hundred feet from the shore, I couldn't see their faces, but I recognized Mikkel's broad shoulders and muscular frame.

"Stop!" I called to the rowers, relief pouring over me. "'Tis them. Go back."

In the same instant, more shouting and the clanking of armor rose into the night air, telling me it was much too perilous to return, that we needed to continue with all haste.

As if recognizing the same urgency, Mikkel dove into the water. Gregor leaped in after him.

Although Irontooth and the others hadn't made an effort to return to the shore, at least they'd stopped rowing. Now the boat bobbed against the gentle waves, and we stared at the sea, waiting for Mikkel and Gregor to appear.

Lantern light flooded the wharf, revealing half a dozen soldiers and the Inquisitor, who was wheezing for breath.

At the grasp of a hand against the stern followed by Mikkel hoisting himself up, I released my pent-up breath and scrambled for him, grabbing his arms and assisting him over the edge. Once securely inside, he reached back for Gregor. Together we hauled him into the boat.

"Go!" Mikkel's breathing was labored. "We have no time to waste."

Irontooth, Toad, and Humphrey had already begun rowing again, and Gregor immediately joined them. From the shore, the shouting continued. The Inquisitor and his men had commandeered two vessels and were already inside and pushing away from the wharf.

They were following us? I'd thought once we were on the open sea, our primary worry would be evading Loch Ness. But perhaps that wouldn't be our greatest challenge on this crossing.

"You'll need to watch the sea for the creature," Mikkel instructed me as he took the position on the opposite side of the boat, already scanning the water. The darkness obscured his features, but his commanding presence calmed my fears. Mikkel wouldn't let anything happen to us.

I turned my attention to the sea too. But I prayed that since it was early in the night, the creature was not yet prowling about the Channel.

The torchlight from the Inquisitor's boats flickered behind us. Every time I glanced toward them, the flames were closer. With six or more men rowing each boat, they could go faster. As if realizing the same, Mikkel grabbed an oar and began to row, still attempting to stay on the lookout for Loch Ness. I did the same, knowing we had to remain well ahead of our pursuers.

As we neared the middle, my arms burned with the effort of rowing, and yet the torchlight drew ever nearer. It wouldn't be long before they were within range to accost us with arrows.

Mikkel darted another look over his shoulder toward the oncoming boats. "Faster. We need to go faster."

Judging by the grunts and heavy breathing from the others, they, like me, were doing as much as they could. But it simply wasn't enough. The Inquisitor would catch up to us before we reached the island, and we would have to battle his men in hand-to-hand combat on the open sea.

"Loch Ness is near." Felicity's warning rang above the thudding of the waves and the rustling of the wind. "There."

Mikkel ceased his rowing and stood, his spear in hand. He followed Felicity's line of attention.

At a whizzing in the air, I called out, "An arrow! Take heed!"

Thankfully, Mikkel had already crouched, and the arrow overshot the boat. As he rose again, another arrow pinged against the wood.

"Stay down," I urged.

But Mikkel raised his spear, his focus on the water.

My heart drummed a warning. He'd placed himself in too much peril all day long. And it was catching up to him.

Something collided with the boat, rocking it so that Mikkel lost his balance. His arms flailed as he attempted to keep his balance. But at another hard thwack, he toppled over and landed in the sea with a splash.

"No!" I scrambled toward the side, panic racing through me. "Mikkel!"

He broke through the surface, spluttering and coughing. I leaned over and held out an arm. He started to swim toward me, but a second later, something long and black twisted around him and dragged him underneath the surface. He disappeared, leaving only bubbles and ripples behind.

Chapter 15

MIKKEL

A SLIPPERY BODY WRAPPED AROUND MY LEGS AND DRAGGED ME down, farther away from the shimmering light on the surface. As I struggled against the eel-like creature, its clutch tightened with each movement. I had mere seconds before its hold would be too secure for me to free myself.

Though I hadn't been able to access my knife, I'd managed to hold on to my spear. I couldn't see through the blackness, but I took aim at the long coil wrapped around my thigh just above my knees.

As the spearhead sank past a scaly layer and penetrated into the flesh, the pressure against my legs loosened enough to yank myself free. I propelled myself up toward the light, kicking my legs and windmilling my arms in an effort to get away.

With my lungs already burning from the lack of air, I couldn't let the serpent entangle me again, or I wouldn't make it. I pumped my legs harder as the creature's long tail slithered around me. Calculating the direction of its movement, I jabbed at the creature again with my spear, this time dragging the blade along its length.

When an inky cloud filled the water around me, I knew I'd injured it. Even then, I didn't let down my guard and launched upward with every ounce of my strength. As I broke through the surface, I gasped for air and filled my lungs just in case the creature snagged me again.

Through the rivulets of water cascading down my face, I glimpsed the torchlight from the Inquisitor's boats, which were much too close.

"Mikkel!" Pearl stretched out over the water, both arms extended.

Fear constricted my throat at the visualization of the creature slithering underneath the vessel, thumping it, and toppling Pearl into the sea. Skillful though she was, she wouldn't have the strength to free herself from Loch Ness. And even if she did, I didn't know if she could swim. Not many could.

"Get back!" I shouted at her. I'd rather Loch Ness take me down again than put Pearl at risk.

She leaned out farther, this time holding out a paddle. "Grab on!"

The first of the boats drew up alongside ours, and shouts rose into the air as Irontooth and the others readied to fight the Inquisitor's men.

At the bump of scaly flesh against my legs, I braced myself for another attack. But the sea serpent glided past, heading in the direction of the boats.

Suddenly desperate, I swung my spear at it, hoping to make contact, needing to distract it and keep it away from Pearl. But the weapon only sliced through the water.

"Hurry!" Pearl called, thrusting out the paddle again.

Once more, all I could see was her plunging into the

water and into Loch Ness's clutches. "Get back into the boat!" I made swift strokes toward her.

She glanced over her shoulder and ducked, an arrow narrowly missing her neck.

As I reached the edge of her paddle, I wanted nothing more than to carry her off to Scania and make sure she was never in this kind of position again. Helplessly, I took hold of her offering and used her strength to add to mine. Within seconds I was at the edge of the boat.

Sudden screams pierced the air. Loch Ness must have knocked another victim into the water. It wasn't Pearl, and I prayed it never would be.

"Praise be." She grabbed my arms and helped haul me into the boat.

I was tempted to berate her, but one of the Inquisitor's guards had fallen overboard, and his comrades were distracted by trying to save him and stave off Loch Ness.

"Let's be on our way!" I called to Irontooth. I needn't have said anything, for he was already rowing. The other men were doing the same. I found a paddle and joined their efforts.

The screaming behind us grew wilder and more panicked before gurgling swallowed it. The remaining guards were shouting at one another to return to shore while the Inquisitor bellowed at them to follow us.

I didn't glance back to gauge their decision. Only one thought pounded through me—that we needed to take advantage of their distraction and put as much distance between both the Inquisitor and Loch Ness as possible.

My pulse slapped in tempo with each stroke, until at last the torchlight as well as the voices faded into blackness. Even then, we didn't slacken on our pace. We rowed silently and swiftly, the whistle of the wind urging us onward.

Through it all, Pearl remained at her oar without resting. I appreciated her tenacity. Most women would have given up. But she was a strong woman, one I could admire. If only I didn't want to strangle her for taking so many risks.

Hours later, without any further encounters with the Inquisitor or Loch Ness, we arrived back at camp and were forthwith surrounded by everyone clamoring to hear about our adventures.

With Felicity at his side, Irontooth was all too willing to provide the details, including the daring rescue of the women at the town center, our race through town, and my escape from Loch Ness.

He made me out to be more of a hero than I wanted. As I tried to answer questions and deflect the admiration, I caught sight of Pearl sneaking away into our cave. From the way she'd lurked at the edge of the gathering and from the tension radiating from her body, she was upset about something.

Was she angry with me? And if so, why? If anyone should be upset, I was more justified than she was.

Excusing myself from the fire pit, I stalked into the cave, my footsteps heavy, my body weary, and my heart burdened.

The light from a lone candle revealed Pearl kneeling in front of an open sack, stuffing food and clothing inside. At the crunch of my steps, she cast me a glance but continued her efforts.

"What are you doing?" I asked.

"I am readying to leave for Warwick."

"I'll go alone without you, as you are too reckless and will get yourself into trouble." I hadn't heretofore considered going alone, but the words spilled out, the culmination of my fear from the past twenty-four hours. I'd had to stand aside and watch her put herself into harm's way too many times, and I didn't know how I could bear it again.

"Reckless? Trouble?" She sat back on her heels, her eyes widening upon me. "And how many times did you just defy death? If anyone is reckless, 'tis you."

"I had everything under control." At least, most of the time.

"As did I," she retorted saucily as she turned her attention back to her packing.

"I want you to stay here. And I shall go to the queen and appeal for Ruby's release into my care." I was putting all my faith in my power as the future king of Scania. I'd give her an opportunity to forge an alliance with Scania in exchange for Ruby. How could she turn it down?

"The queen wants me and will not be satisfied until she has me."

"Then all the more reason to remain behind."

Pearl stood then and spun. "This is my battle, not yours."

"The day we spoke our vows to each other, your battles became mine."

Pearl tilted her head, regarding me with serious eyes. "I do not know what the queen intends, but she will not rest until she has what she seeks."

I started across the cave, rounding the hearth that

was cold and lifeless. As I approached, Pearl crossed her arms as though to shield herself. From what? From me?

Surely she sensed my loyalty to her by now. "I'll not let her have you."

"You may not have a choice."

When I stopped in front of her, I wanted to wrap my arms around her and hold her tight, especially when she turned the full force of her gaze upon me, her green eyes so luminous and beautiful above the line of her veil. I started to reach for her, but she held up a hand. "I shall not let you touch me and attempt to mold me into doing as you wish."

"I only do so because I care about you." The words slipped out before I could filter them. Nevertheless, once spoken, I was relieved she knew the truth.

Her eyes flickered with accusation. "You could have died today."

I took a step closer so I almost touched her, but I refrained. "Does that mean you care about me too?"

"It means pack your bags swiftly if you do not wish for me to leave you behind."

Although she might not admit she was beginning to care about me too, I sensed she'd been as worried about me during the battle with the Inquisitor and Loch Ness as I had been about her.

"We'll rest a few hours," I insisted. "Then we'll start off before dawn."

She took a breath as though she might protest, but then she nodded. "Very well."

We stood face-to-face, neither of us moving. My fingers itched with the need to reach for the strings of her veil. I wanted to untie them, let the silk fall away, and prove to myself and to her that whatever deformities or scars she was hiding didn't matter. I'd failed to convey that after our kiss and wanted to make up for my mistake.

Although I wanted to accept her and value those blemishes because they were what had shaped her into the strong woman she'd become, was I truly ready to see her flaws? Could I do so without reacting? I wanted to think I could, but was I strong enough?

Even as I longed to break down the last barriers that stood between us, I knew that for now, the veil could keep her safe from recognition, especially as we traveled into Warwick amongst people who would more readily identify her as the princess she was.

Furthermore, I wanted her to be the one to remove the veil of her own free will. And I sensed she would only do so when she felt as though she could trust me completely. After all that had happened with her mother, her trust was the one thing that would be hardest to earn but would also be the most valuable.

Thus, I would bide my time and leave the veil in place.

Chapter 16

Pearl

The voyage to Warwick took longer than I wanted. But I respected Mikkel's desire for caution. We sailed south in the calm waters of Oceanus along the coastline of the Great Isle, making our way at night and then finding secluded places to hide during the day.

Before departing, Mikkel and I had approached Irontooth with our plans. Though Mikkel reassured our leader he'd return within a month to finish his Testing, I'd sensed resignation from Irontooth, as though he realized, just as I did, that this new mission made the rescue of the women from Fife look like child's play.

Even so, Irontooth had insisted on giving us a purse of silver that we could use to purchase supplies and food along the way. I privately vowed to repay Irontooth someday for his kindness, though I knew not how.

A week passed by the time we docked at the Cambrian Lowlands in Warwick. There Mikkel secured mounts from local sheep farmers. Then we set out with all haste to reach the woodland that bordered the mountains, anxious to find cover within the forest.

During our journey, whenever we needed anything, Mikkel insisted that Gregor and I wait in hiding as he conducted the bargaining. While he didn't say so, I knew he was afraid people would take more notice of me because of my veil and Gregor for his scars. And we didn't need any undue attention. He also insisted I wear my veil to hide my identity as Princess Pearl. I understood his reasoning and agreed, but a part of me wondered if he was glad for the excuses, so he could put off looking at the real me for as long as possible.

Had I only imagined the desire I'd seen in Mikkel's eyes our last night on the Isle of Outcasts? I'd almost believed for a few seconds that he didn't care anymore what I looked like, and that he might even reach up and remove my veil.

"I care about you." I hadn't imagined his words, and they stayed close to my heart. I cared about him too, and as we traveled long hours, I cherished him all the more for our easy conversations as well as deep discussions. Though we shared many things in common and our friendship deepened, I couldn't squelch my growing disappointment that he showed no interest in seeing behind my veil.

Whenever I thought about the kisses we'd exchanged that night in Fife, I wanted to pull down my veil and show him he had nothing to be afraid of. But the longer he delayed initiating the removal, the more I resolved to wait to reveal myself to him until he asked it of me, until he was ready to accept me completely for who I was as a person and not for how I looked.

Another week elapsed before we reached the foothills and the more populated area of Warwick. Each passing day brought an increasing sense of unease. Though we didn't meet many people, those we came across were frightened, withdrawn, and even hostile. Towns were quiet, and the fields to the southeast lay deserted of the many peasant laborers who worked them in the summer.

By the time we were a two days' ride from Kensington, my apprehension had only grown.

"I do not understand," I said, as I rode next to Mikkel. The village we'd just skirted had been abandoned. The thatched huts were dark, doors open, shutters broken or hanging by one hinge, and garden beds overgrown with weeds. "'Tis as if a plague has struck the people."

"No one has made mention of disease." Mikkel's eyes narrowed as he scanned the darkness of the surrounding countryside. Always alert, Mikkel used the scant light from the stars and moon to guide us. From behind, Gregor, too, was ever aware of our surroundings.

The scent of a campfire hovered in the air, signaling the presence of others in the area, and yet the wooded trail kept us hidden. Old fir and hemlock mixed with seedlings of the new growth among the large boulders and crags, shielding us as we rested by day and providing security for our travels by night.

"A year ago, the land was well populated." Something had happened during the time I'd been gone from Warwick. And whatever it was didn't bode well.

At a nearby woman's scream, I reined in my mount.

Mikkel's horse shied next to me, and Gregor already had his sword drawn. We waited unmoving, all of us, attempting to decipher the meaning of the scream.

Raucous laughter drifted into the air followed by more screaming.

"Someone is in trouble." I shifted my mount toward the sound.

Mikkel held out a gloved hand. "I shall ride ahead and scout the situation."

"Should we not stay together?" I whispered with a glance around at the dark shadows of the woodland. "Surely we are safer that way?"

Mikkel hesitated and exchanged a glance with Gregor. "Very well, but you and Gregor must remain out of sight."

I nudged my horse forward, already veering in the direction of the laughter. Mikkel pushed ahead of me, taking the lead, and Gregor formed the rear, silent but seeming to see everything.

The light of flames guided us to a camp. As we reached the outskirts, we could see a group of men with long, unkempt hair and scraggly beards terrorizing what appeared to be a family. One of them had pinned a woman's arms behind her back and had a knife against her throat. Two others were holding a man between them and another was beating him. Several young children ducked behind a cart and watched, their eyes rounded with fear.

Without waiting for Mikkel or Gregor, I charged forward, my bow fitted with an arrow. I let it fly toward the man threatening the woman, then readied another and aimed it at the other perpetrator. He howled as the arrow pierced into his shoulder.

Mikkel broke into the camp ahead of me, wielding his spear in one hand and knife in the other. Within seconds, the men fell to the ground, unconscious or too debilitated to fight back.

He jumped off his horse and dropped onto the largest of the men, spear thrust against his chest. "Who are you and what are you doing?"

The burly man beneath Mikkel's boots released a snarl of laughter. "I thought everyone knew who we were."

I remained on the edge of the camp, out of the full light of the campfire, but Gregor had wasted no time in dismounting and beginning the process of disarming and binding the bedraggled men who, upon closer examination, had yellowed, emaciated skin, hollowed eyes, and gray broken teeth.

They looked as though they'd been sorely abused themselves. But by whom and for what reason?

The woman, now free, had hurried to her children and now huddled with them behind the cart, drawing them into her arms and comforting them.

The husband cradled his stomach, likely sustaining cracked ribs if not a broken arm.

Mikkel shifted his glance to me, as though reassuring himself I was safe. In that instant, his prisoner managed to slip a knife from his belt and raised it toward Mikkel's leg.

"On your left!" I shouted, my pulse spurting.

Mikkel jabbed the spear into the man's arm with a force that thrust it to the ground and pinned it in place. The man cried out and released his hold on the knife.

Digging his spear deeper into the man's flesh, Mikkel glared down at him. "Tell me who you are and what your business is here assaulting this family."

"We're slaves," he ground out, "set free from the mine pits by Prince Vilmar."

Mikkel grew deathly still. "Prince Vilmar?"

My racing heartbeat came to an abrupt halt.

During the past long days of traveling, Mikkel hadn't mentioned contacting Vilmar. As a man of honor, Mikkel probably had no wish to interfere with his brother's training in any way.

"Prince Vilmar is from Scania," the slave said, even as he grimaced from pain.

"Yes, I know where Prince Vilmar is from," Mikkel said irritably. "Why did he set the slaves free from the mine pits?"

These were former slaves? I assessed the leader and then the other men, whom Gregor had now bound. From their skeletal condition and sallow skin, I had no doubt they'd been imprisoned. But the one time I'd gone with my mother and her priests for the prayer ceremony at the mine pits, the slaves hadn't been this depraved. Though I'd been appalled to learn many slaves lost limbs due to accidents and rat bites, I'd also been struck by how normal most of them looked, like ordinary people, not common criminals. Not like these men.

When I'd questioned one of the priests, he'd explained the slaves were made up of criminals convicted of lesser offenses. The worst prisoners—the most violent and vilest—were condemned to the dungeons and eventually put to death.

Perhaps over the year I'd been gone, the queen had grown more desperate for slaves to labor in her mine and decided to send even the worst the criminals there too. If so, at least one of them would likely have lost a limb. And as far as I could tell, their arms and legs were intact.

"Tell me what you know of Prince Vilmar." Mikkel shifted the spear blade to a new spot on his prisoner's arm.

"He's wanted by the queen," the prisoner cried out, "for leading a revolt at the mine pits."

Mikkel glared down at the man.

I studied the prisoners again. Something wasn't right. "You cannot trust what these criminals tell you."

"I'm telling the truth! The queen has put a bounty on Prince Vilmar's head. He's wanted dead or alive."

The peasant man who'd gone to his wife and children now stepped forward. "We don't know what be truth anymore."

"I give you leave to speak of what you've heard." Mikkel gave the peasant man a cursory glance but kept his focus on his prisoner as Gregor began to bind him.

"No one knows why the prince was workin' as a slave in the mine," the peasant said. "But he released the prisoners and came to Kensington on Midsummer's Eve."

"He captured Grendel," the woman said, awe tinting her voice.

A tremor ran up my spine at the very thought that the monster was gone along with the yearly sacrifice of the fairest maiden. "Truly?"

The woman nodded eagerly. "The prince locked Grendel in a cage and sent him away from Warwick."

"To Scania?" Mikkel asked.

"Aye. Under heavy guard."

I whispered a silent prayer of thanksgiving. I didn't

know how or why Vilmar had accomplished so great a feat, but already I liked him. After the years of terror Grendel had unleashed in Warwick, Vilmar should have become a national hero. Not a man wanted dead or alive.

As though coming to the same conclusion, Mikkel's brows came together in a deep scowl. "Why would the queen punish Prince Vilmar for eliminating this monster?"

The prisoner snorted. "I already told you. He released the slaves from the mine pits."

The peasant man wrapped an arm around his children. "And now the criminals be runnin' through the land plunderin' and destroyin'."

"We lost our home already." The woman clung to her husband, her expression desperate. "And these men would take the little we have left."

Mikkel stood rigidly. "Has the queen not sent her knights to restore order?"

"We haven't seen nary a one since Midsummer's Eve."

That was at least six weeks ago, if my calculations were correct.

Mikkel's eyes teemed with questions, likely the same questions I had, ones I couldn't begin to answer.

"Did Prince Vilmar return to the mine pits?" Mikkel asked.

"No one knows where he is." The prisoner released a sneering laugh. "If we did, we sure wouldn't tell you and let you collect the reward."

Mikkel studied the prisoner a moment. "Tell me, why would Prince Vilmar risk his life to save this land from Grendel's ravages only to free criminals to roam around and ravage in the monster's stead?"

The firelight reflected off the prisoner's face, revealing a smirk.

"You were not in the mine pits." I wanted to move into the firelight but forced myself to remain where I was. "Were you?"

"Aye, of course we were."

"Then tell me how you left Slave Town." There was one way in and out of the mine pits—a suspension bridge made of ropes and wooden slats. It hung over a deep ravine and was frightening to cross. It had swayed the entire time I was on it, and I'd feared at any moment I might fall to my death.

The prisoner hesitated. "I can't tell you now, can I? Or more prisoners would end up revolting."

"You cannot tell me because you have never been there." I shifted in my saddle, wishing I could get down and wrest the truth from him.

"I've been there. I swear it."

I locked gazes with Mikkel. "He is lying."

"What shall I do to elicit the truth from him? Skin him alive?"

Mikkel would never do such a thing, but I played along with him. "Yes, but scalp him first."

"Very well, my lady. Your wish is my command." He unsheathed his knife and stalked toward the prisoner now tied to one of the trees. Mikkel's blade was longer and sharper than most, and it glinted in the firelight. Upon reaching the prisoner, Mikkel grabbed a fistful of the man's hair at his temple and then pressed the knife to the spot.

The prisoner screamed—more from fear than pain, for Mikkel had drawn only a scant amount of blood.

"You're right. We weren't in the mine pits. We were in the dungeons beneath the palace."

Mikkel withdrew his knife a fraction. "Who released you and why?"

"The queen's guards. They told us we were free and to do what we would, but that we had to tell people we'd escaped from the mine pits."

Mikkel pulled his knife away, then thrust the man's head back as though disgusted with him.

I was more disgusted with my mother than with these criminals. She'd set them free? And for what reason? Did the reason even matter? Was there any excuse for giving such dangerous criminals license to *do what they would*? And why would she want to cause Vilmar distress, especially after he'd put an end to the dreaded ritual that had cast a pall over Warwick for so many years?

Mikkel mounted his horse and gave instructions for the family regarding the criminals. When we were on our way, Mikkel rode silently. I sensed his tempestuous mood and so remained quiet as well, letting my thoughts gallop far ahead. What was my mother thinking?

The truth was, I'd never been able to understand her. Especially not her plot to have me murdered.

Shortly after I turned eighteen, she had planned a hunting trip with courtiers and friends. Only two weeks before the Choosing Ball, I'd assumed it was one last gift to me, that she suspected as well as I did that there was every real chance I'd be sacrificed to Grendel. I hadn't been overly frightened by the prospect, had decided if someone must die, then I would give my life. I only regretted having to leave Ruby behind.

I'd started the hunting trip determined to make the most of my favorite pastime. Little had I known the queen had arranged for one of the royal huntsmen to coerce me away from the others with tales of a beautiful white buck. I went with him, only to have him creep up behind me and start squeezing my neck.

Thankfully, another of the huntsmen had been suspicious and followed us. He knocked out his companion from behind, warned me of the queen's scheming, and told me to run away and not come back. I was indebted to that lone huntsman for looking out for me and prayed he had escaped the queen's wrath when she learned I hadn't died after all.

I had to accept the truth no matter how much it hurt. She'd never loved me. Not even when I'd been a little girl. I'd always fallen short of earning her favor and attention. Mostly she'd used me like an object on display, having Ruby and me trail her in our glorious gowns and brilliant jewels as an extension of her glamour.

However, in the last few years, I'd consistently drawn the attention *away* from her rather than *to* her. But was jealousy enough to lead to murder? Especially of one's daughter?

"Why does your mother want to kill my brother?" Mikkel's voice broke through my reverie. Accusation dripped from every word.

My attention snapped to him. Though the darkness of the woodland shrouded him, I could sense the rigidness of his posture.

Did he think I was connected with my mother's scheming against Vilmar? Or that I was in some way to blame? My ire flared to life as rapidly as dry windfall catching a flyaway spark. "And why do you think I would know such information? Have you forgotten that my mother wants to kill me too?"

I kicked my mount into a trot, moving ahead of Mikkel. Now that we were so close to Kensington, I knew the forests well. I'd hunted this land oft enough over the years with my father. I had many good memories of my adventures with him, which only served to heighten my sorrow.

"She is angry with Vilmar for capturing Grendel," Mikkel stated, his voice still hard. "Therefore, I conclude she had need of the madman in some way. You must tell me what it is."

Had the queen needed Grendel? I'd always believed her resistance to capturing the monster had to do with her unwillingness to put my father at risk. But she could have assigned her toughest warriors to the task, could she not? Why hadn't she?

"Speak the truth, Pearl. I must know everything."

"And I have told you everything."

"Vilmar has discovered her secret for needing Grendel," Mikkel continued, "and she seeks his death so he won't tell anyone else."

"'Tis possible." Mikkel's observations were astute as usual. That he could so quickly analyze information and draw conclusions never failed to amaze me. And now curiosity replaced my irritation.

"You must tell me her secret," Mikkel insisted.

"I have no knowledge of a secret."

"Does this have something to do with her obsession with the white stone and alchemy?"

"I cannot see how."

"You must have some inkling."

"I have been honest with you about everything." Once the words were out, guilt slapped me hard across my face. I hadn't been honest with him about my appearance.

He didn't contradict my statement, but his ensuing silence indicated that he was thinking of my veil too. Perhaps he was justified in his mistrust. Perhaps we both still needed to learn to trust each other.

Should I remove my veil and tell him the truth about myself at this very moment? I reached for the strings that held the covering in place. If I showed him my face, would he treat me like all the other men I'd known? Seeing only my beauty and focusing on that to the exclusion of everything else?

He was the first man who valued me as a friend, accepted my ideas, and listened to my opinions.

I let my hand drop back to the reins. I loved the camaraderie we'd developed, especially over the past fortnight of traveling, and I didn't want that to change. Not yet. Once we had Ruby, I'd tell him the truth then.

For now, what would it hurt to keep the veil in place a little longer?

"If Vilmar has made an enemy of the queen," Mikkel said, "will she consider me a foe as well?"

"'Tis quite likely she will regard you with ill will."

Mikkel muttered something about Vilmar being foolish. "Let us pray she will not reject my request for Ruby on account of Vilmar."

My heart stumbled a beat at the thought of Mikkel seeking an audience with the queen. "You cannot go before her now that your brother is her enemy."

"I'm willing to take the risk for Ruby's sake."

I shook my head even though the darkness

concealed the motion. "No. If the queen realizes you have any connection either to me or Vilmar, she will most definitely hold you as her prisoner."

"I'm not planning to tell her you are my wife. Only that you have sought refuge in Scania and that you request sanctuary for Ruby as well."

"Even if you say nothing about our union, she will hold you for ransom on account of Vilmar."

"In exchange for Ruby, I will offer her the one thing she has longed for that my father denied her. The chance to forge an alliance with Scania once I become king."

I paused. Would the queen accept such an offer? "'Tis no secret she wishes to gain the friendship of other nations so that when she attempts to reclaim Mercia, no one will protest or come to Mercia's aid."

"She also knows that an alliance with Scania can provide valuable resources she may need during times of war, especially ships."

The queen had talked of reuniting Mercia and Warwick for many years but lacked the resources to do so. Mikkel's offer of Scania's friendship and the prospect of gaining well-crafted vessels would entice her. But would it be enough?

The plodding hooves of our horses filled the air around us along with the soft trill of crickets. I released a tense breath. No matter what we chose to do, the way would be fraught with peril. "I believe the wisest course of action is to remain steadfast with what I have planned all along, and that is to sneak into the castle, kidnap Ruby, and steal her away before anyone can report it."

"If any kidnapping is to be done, Gregor and I shall

be the ones to do it, not you."

"I know the castle better than anyone—"

"I shall attempt to negotiate for Ruby's release first, and if that fails, Gregor and I will steal her away." From the stubborn ring of his tone and after what had happened in Fife, I knew Mikkel intended to sacrifice his own safety and well-being once more. But this time, I couldn't let him.

Whether he liked it or not, I would be the one going in to do the rescuing. Hopefully, by the time he realized my plans, I'd already be in and out of the castle with Ruby in tow.

Chapter 17

MIKKEL

FROM THE TOP OF THE WINDING MOUNTAIN ROAD THAT LED TO the royal palace, I gazed down onto Kensington, which spread out a league or more from the foothills into the fertile plains beyond. Like the area we'd traversed, it, too, showed signs of the rampaging and pillaging we'd witnessed in the countryside.

Even though the final two nights of traveling yielded no further encounters with rogue criminals, every step that drew us closer to the capital increased my eagerness to confront the queen. If she could so callously free her worst criminals in order to vilify Vilmar, she clearly cared nothing for her people.

My gut cinched again, as it had since I'd learned of his plight. I could only pray he was unharmed and had found a safe place away from the queen's clutches.

I still didn't understand why he'd decided to leave his Testing to fight Grendel. It was noble of him. Maybe he'd made plans like mine, hoping to return to his Testing, but circumstances hadn't turned out the way he expected.

I shoved aside the unease such thoughts brought me. I was different than Vilmar. I operated with more logic and strategic planning. Like now. I wouldn't fail in my mission.

With a glance toward the setting sun, I pushed away from the half stone wall that overlooked the city.

"What do you suggest next, Your Highness?" Gregor whispered, glancing up the last stretch of road to the gatehouse. Except for a few beggars along the way and some travelers descending from the palace, the cobbled road had been mostly deserted during our climb.

"I suggest we continue as planned." I knew Gregor worried that people we met would shun him for his scars and his eye patch, but his face was hidden in his hood. And when we approached the guards on duty, I would do most of the talking. They likely wouldn't even notice him. And if they decided not to allow him to enter, then I would have to proceed alone.

"Maybe we should wait for morn to approach the queen."

I paused, taking in the gatehouse ahead with its imposing towers as well as the enormous castle beyond that was half-built into the cliff walls. Turrets rose high as if to compete with the mountain range upon which the fortress was built. The crenellations and merlons of the battlements were formed into diamonds, and the arrow slits in the towers were shaped like crosses.

In some ways, the royal residence set against the backdrop of the mountains reminded me of Bergenborg Castle, where my family had spent winters for as long as I could remember. But something about this city and Warwick set me on edge. No matter the similarities in geography between countries, the leadership made all the difference. And Queen Margery's rule had created a realm where fear and hardship abounded rather than peace and prosperity.

Now that I'd witnessed Warwick's fate under the queen, I prayed I would never forget to put the needs of my people above my own.

"Let us continue onward." I lengthened my stride. "The sooner we conduct our business, the sooner we can leave."

I feared the more time we lingered in Warwick, the greater the chances someone would recognize Pearl. Even more, I feared that if we waited until morn, Pearl would demand to join me inside the castle. As it was, after arguing, she'd glared at me but thankfully agreed to wait in the chamber we rented above an obscure tavern until our return. I couldn't come back without Ruby and thus disappoint her. To ensure her cooperation, I'd enlisted the tavern owner to watch her door and stop her if she tried to leave.

All the while I'd walked through town and up the path to the castle, I'd had the strange feeling something wasn't right, that Pearl had acquiesced too easily. It was just one more reason to finish our business with the queen hastily.

As we hiked the last distance to the gatehouse, the setting sun glinted off a thick double iron gate. Gregor stopped a distance away, but I approached and was surprised to find both gates already closed. I peered up into first one tower, then the other. I didn't see anyone, but I had no doubt the guards on duty were well aware of my presence. "I would like to request admittance—"

An arrow sliced through the air, and I dodged out of the way as it hit the spot where I'd just stood. "Leave at once or the next arrow will find its mark."

I had no choice but to back away, all the while keeping

my attention on the arrow slits in the tower.

Gregor and I retreated down the mountain path, walking backward and never once taking our sight from the gatehouse until we rounded the corner and were no longer within shooting range.

Once we were safe, I stopped and frowned. "I should have surmised from the scarcity of people climbing the path that the gate wouldn't be open." I didn't give Gregor the chance to say that he'd told me so. Instead, I approached a beggar resting with his back against the hillside. "What time does the gatehouse close every day?"

The beggar held out a sagging cap, peering straight ahead with empty eye sockets. He jangled the few coins already inside his cap, as though to suggest payment before he would divulge the information I wanted.

I nodded at Gregor, who took a farthing from his pocket and dropped it into the hat.

"Obliged," said the man, revealing several missing front teeth.

"The gate?" I persisted.

"It be closing at Vespers every day."

The cathedral bells had rung for the six o'clock hour of prayer as we'd set out from the tavern. Surely if this beggar knew the castle's timetable, then Pearl was aware of it as well. She should have warned me we wouldn't make it to the top in time to enter.

"When does the gate open on the morrow?"

The beggar pressed his lips together and shook his hat. Stifling a sigh of irritation, I motioned for Gregor. At the clank of another coin dropping into the hat, the beggar smiled, once again showing his broken and crooked teeth. "The gate opens at the ringing of Terce."

I should have guessed as much. Though I was eager to

negotiate for Ruby and start on my way back to the island to finish my Testing, what was one more night? Tomorrow would be here soon enough, and I would accomplish our mission then.

Meanwhile, I would have to find a way to placate Pearl. She would be sorely disappointed at not getting to see her sister tonight. But hopefully, she would understand we could do naught.

As we retraced our steps down the mountainside and through the city, darkness crept over the streets. Along with it came more of the thievery and thuggery we'd witnessed elsewhere. Gregor and I fended off two different attackers, hid on several occasions, and came to the aid of others even more oft.

It didn't take long to realize that lawlessness reigned over the city the same way it did the countryside. No place in Warwick was safe, which was all the more reason to leave the country as soon as possible.

Why hadn't Pearl told us about the castle gate closing time? The question nagged me. And by the time we reached the remote corner of the city where we'd taken our room, my pulse was racing with a strange rhythm of dread.

As I burst through the tavern door, the few patrons paused, weapons drawn, wariness upon their countenances. After reassurances from the proprietor that they had nothing to fear from Gregor and me, they sheathed their knives and returned to their meals.

The tavern owner assured me Pearl hadn't left her room. Nevertheless, I took the stairs two at a time, gave a cursory knock to our chamber door, then threw it open wide. My heartbeat slowed to an agonizing crawl. She was nowhere in sight. "Pearl," I hissed, praying she was merely hiding.

Silence met my request. I heard only the murmur of voices and clink of dishes from below along with a distant crash followed by shouting and cursing.

I crossed to the bed that was rumpled but otherwise undisturbed. I surveyed underneath to find dust mites and the dark glowing eyes of a mouse. As I straightened, frustration poured into my veins.

"She's gone," I whispered to Gregor who stood in the doorway.

Throwing off his hood, he scanned the room and then the short hallway that led to several other chambers. "Do you think someone recognized and took her?"

The thread of anxiety in Gregor's voice wove itself into my worry. "If she'd gone unwillingly, we would see signs of a scuffle." As it was, everything was untouched and in the same order we'd found it when we first arrived. In fact, from the neatness of the chamber, she hadn't stayed long.

I spun, stalked to the door, and pushed past him, hoping she'd simply stepped outside for a breath of air. But as I searched the premises and the surrounding alley and buildings, including the stable with our horses, I couldn't find a trace of her, and no one I questioned had seen her. Since her horse was penned with the others and resting contentedly, she must still be in the city. And if she remained in the city, my gut told me she'd be in only one place. The royal castle.

But with the entrance on the mountaintop above the city, we would have seen her during our climb up and back. Unless she'd hidden until we'd descended and were on our way back to the tavern. Though the guards at the gatehouse had been unwilling to give us the slightest consideration, not even a moment to reveal my identity, they would recognize Pearl and allow her admittance.

Unless she knew another entrance to the fortress . . .

As we returned to the tavern, both dread and apprehension twisted together in a tight plait that fastened around my neck like a noose. I sank to a bench at the table across from Gregor and buried my face in my hands.

She'd left for the palace to redeem Ruby without me. I had no doubt she'd done it to protect me, hadn't wanted to put me at risk. But now she'd put her own life in jeopardy, and I couldn't bear the thought.

At the thud of mugs on the table, I raised my head long enough to thank the proprietor as well as take a long drink. Though my pulse pounded with the need to go after Pearl, I couldn't devise a plan. My usual quick thinking and decisiveness had deserted me in my greatest hour of need, and all I could think about was how hopeless and helpless I was to stop her.

Whether she'd gotten into the castle through the main gatehouse or a hidden passageway, I was locked out for the night with no way of getting inside. I would have to wait until morn to request an audience with the queen.

Now all I could envision was Pearl creeping closer to the trap the queen had laid out for her. For surely that's what this was. The queen was taking advantage of the sisterly bond, a bond that would drive Pearl to go to any lengths to save Ruby.

Though Pearl might have the advantage of stealth and was proficient with her weapons, the queen would keep Ruby under heavy guard. Every entrance and exit would be carefully monitored. If Pearl managed to make it all the way to Ruby, it would be only because the queen allowed it.

Once the queen had Pearl, would she try to kill her?

Every muscle in my body protested the prospect of losing her. The thought should have surprised me. After all, breaking with tradition and returning to Scania with a wife would cause a disturbance amongst the Lagting.

Yet, even with the heavy censure awaiting me, my heart ached at the prospect of not being together with Pearl. I couldn't deny the powerful connection I had with her or the attraction that had grown with each passing day. Aside from how much I desired her, I'd also never had so deep a friendship with anyone, man or woman. And I couldn't abide the thought of losing so close a friend. In fact, the possibility of life without Pearl filled me with such melancholy I wanted to weep.

I pushed aside my mug, lowered my head, and prayed. At the moment, prayer was the only weapon I had.

Chapter
18

Pearl

The passageway was steeper than I remembered. And longer.

I'd been but a wee child the last time I used the tunnel with my father, and my memories were tempered by time. Moreover, unlike the tension of the present, our exploring had been carefree as we pretended we were escaping from the castle far above while it was under attack from a dangerous enemy. I'd raced up and down the winding trails while my father chased after, the low ceilings and narrow walls impeding his movement as they were now doing to mine.

In hindsight, I couldn't help but wonder if my father's motivation for taking me to the passageway had been much deeper than mere child's play. Had he been preparing me for a real siege? Or had he worried I'd have a need to escape the queen one day?

Regardless, I was grateful I could get into the castle without having to go through the main gatehouse.

While I might have been able to use my veil to disguise myself for a short time, eventually someone would have recognized me and alerted the queen to my presence.

Now I hoped I could enter and exit undetected during the dark of night with fewer servants and soldiers to evade.

I'd expected a guard at the entrance in the underground burial chambers of the cathedral, but no one had been there, not even the nuns who lived in the abbey above the vault. It hadn't taken overlong to pick the locks securing the hidden door. But I accomplished the feat with one of my hairpins, grateful for the many ways Irontooth had prepared me for this return.

I paused and held out my torch, straining to see ahead. My neck and shoulders ached from stooping for so long. But after an hour of climbing, I could finally see the end.

Releasing a taut breath, I allowed myself the first respite since I'd snuck out the upstairs window of the tavern after darkness had fallen. No doubt Mikkel was furious with me for leaving. And no doubt he'd guessed I was setting off on a rescue of Ruby without him. I hated the prospect that he was angry and perhaps disappointed in me.

Nevertheless, I preferred to keep him alive and experience his wrath rather than to risk him falling into the queen's hands. That meant I had to return to the tavern with Ruby by first light before he and Gregor left for the castle once more.

I braced a hand against the cold stone wall and glanced back down the winding tunnel, now dark and silent. My torchlight illuminated spiderwebs, rat droppings, and crumbling stone. The passageway hadn't been used in years, perhaps not since my father's and my escapades. Did the queen even remember it was here? If she did, I hoped she didn't know Father had revealed it to me and consequently have guards posted at the top.

With my back hunched, I scrambled up the last incline. As I rounded a final bend, I ducked under more dusty spiderwebs. The passageway widened and ended at several steps leading to a hatch in the stone ceiling. Though the wooden slats appeared easy to lift, it was locked from the other side and led directly to another hatch concealed under a carpet in the antechamber off the great hall. At the late hour, I prayed no one was in the small room my mother used to meet privately with advisors.

For long seconds, I listened for voices or sounds from above. Even though silence greeted me, it was still possible for guards to be lying in wait. I wouldn't know for certain until I pushed up the rug.

Unwilling to let uncertainty stop me, I thrust my knife into the hatch and chipped away at the old wood until my fingers were blistered and arms were trembling from weariness. After making a hole large enough to squeeze my hand through, I fumbled for the lock and blindly worked at picking it.

The process was slow, and with each failed attempt, I grew more flustered. Would I need to return to the tavern and admit my failure? Perhaps I'd have no choice but to follow Mikkel's plan. Certainly it had some merit.

And yet, I couldn't shake the fear that the queen would hold Mikkel hostage to draw in Vilmar, the same way she was holding Ruby in order to gain me. I couldn't chance letting her have another person I loved.

My fingers came to a halt against the rusted lock. Did I love Mikkel?

I shook my head. No, I couldn't love him. I cared about him and had developed a bond with him. But I surely hadn't fallen in love. I needed him. That's all. Ruby and I needed his aid in reaching the safety of a new life in Scania. Once there, I'd do what I'd planned all along—give him an annulment. Wouldn't I?

"Focus," I whispered, as I pressed the hairpin against the inner lock mechanism once more. I slowed my motion, probed harder, and felt the slight click that meant I'd jarred it loose.

I wasted no further time. I pried the lock away, slid the hatch aside, and then pressed on the second hatch just inches above the first. It didn't budge, and I prayed no one had moved a piece of furniture onto it. If so, I wouldn't have a chance of entering this way.

I heaved again, and this time the wooden slats lifted slightly. Praise be. Nothing too heavy sat on the hatch. Though my arms burned with the pressure of the exertion, I managed to slide the hatch away little by little until I'd made an opening big enough for my body. Extinguishing the torch and leaving it behind, I crawled up and underneath the rug until I bumped into the legs of a chair. I halted, not wanting to tip anything and cause a clatter.

I shifted my direction and exited from underneath the carpet in a different location. Quickly and quietly, I placed the hatch back over the opening and then situated the rug. If anyone came into the room before I made my escape with Ruby, at least they wouldn't be any wiser for my intrusion.

Though I was nowhere near Ruby yet, I felt as though I'd accomplished the hardest part of my mission by getting inside undetected. I had many more obstacles to overcome, but the rest of the distance to the east tower and Ruby's chambers was familiar. I'd already plotted my route and would stick to unlit servants' corridors as I made my way there.

As I took a deep breath, I could almost smell the waft of my mother's rich perfume and picture her face—flawless and beautiful and regal. And yet so cold and uncaring.

What had happened to cause her to lose her love for her family? Had she lost it when she'd had the falling out with her father and sister? She rarely talked about her family, particularly her twin sister, Leandra. I'd never known my aunt, since she'd died giving birth to her only child, my cousin Aurora.

However, I'd gleaned enough to know my mother felt as though their father, King Alfred, had always favored Leandra. She claimed he'd given Leandra the better inheritance by bestowing upon her the kingdom of Mercia as well as an ancient set of three keys that unlocked a fabled treasure.

How could a treasure—that may or may not exist—be better than a gem mine already producing jewels? Or how was Mercia better, since it was smaller?

I suspected Mother's hurt stemmed more from feeling unloved than from an inferior inheritance. And at times, I also suspected feeling rejected by her family had caused her to close herself off to her children. Perhaps she unconsciously believed if she didn't love anyone, then she wouldn't be hurt again.

Whatever the case, I'd stopped having any sympathy for her the day she'd tried to have me killed. The last vestiges of respect and love had vanished. Henceforth, I didn't care what became of her, only that I could free Ruby from her control.

As I crept across the antechamber toward the door, the floor squeaked. I halted and waited, listening for the approach of footsteps from the noble knights, squires, and pages resting amongst the rushes of the great hall.

After a moment of silence, I expelled a breath and continued. Thankfully, the door didn't squeal on its hinges as I opened it. I stayed low and slipped along the perimeter of the room with my back pressed against the cold wall. The hearth fire glowed low, adding enough light that I could make my way without bumping into anyone or anything.

When I was close to the bottom of the double marble stairway that led to the second floor, a nearby dog lifted its head and looked in my direction. When it stood and released a low huff, I froze.

One of the pages murmured something to the dog before he rolled over and went back to sleep.

I remained motionless, waiting for someone else to sit up and spot me. But only the dog lumbered over, its snout in the air. It gave another soft bark, then wagged its tail. Did it recognize me? Or at the very least remember my scent?

It sniffed my legs before it plopped down, peering up at me with its ears cocked. I held out my hand and let it sniff me more closely.

"Stay," I whispered as I started up the stairs.

It watched with curious eyes each step I took up the broad stairway, but it made no more noise or effort to follow me. When I reached the landing, I ducked behind the balcony where my mother presided over the Choosing Ball each Midsummer's Eve.

Though I'd never attended the event, I oft peeked from the hallway, glimpsing the fairest maidens in the land dancing in their emerald gowns. The music had been festive, the clothing beautiful, and the decorations lavish. Though the queen required everyone to smile and be happy, nothing was ever able to mask the fear in each of the faces. I'd sensed that fear as palpably as if it had been a living force hovering above the gathering.

Now, as I slipped into the passageway, my thoughts turned to Mikkel's brother Vilmar. If he was anything like Mikkel, then he was a good and brave man, and I hoped one day I'd have the chance to thank him for capturing Grendel.

I still didn't understand why my mother hadn't been more pleased by Vilmar's defeat of the monster. Mikkel's suspicions from the previous night had stayed with me. And the more I thought about them, the more I agreed. The queen had been using Grendel for her own purposes, something to do with her alchemy. Since it was the most important thing to her, everything always had to do with her alchemy. Always.

Sconces glimmered at intervals down the long hallway. Though I didn't see any guards on duty, I stayed along the edge until I reached a doorway leading to the servants' corridors.

Most of the castle staff would be asleep, but I remained alert as I raced through the narrow halls and reached the tower housing Ruby's chambers. Once there, I peeked in the direction of her door. It was guarded. The queen was attempting to prevent Ruby from escaping—or perhaps had anticipated a rescue effort.

I'd suspected that would be the case. With haste, I unrolled the habit I'd pilfered from the abbey and donned it over my garments. While the gray undyed wool was scratchy and stifling and several sizes too big, it would have to do.

I hesitated but a moment before I removed the veil that had been my shield for many months. I couldn't keep it over my face if I hoped to pass as a nun. Instead, I wound the nun's wimple around my head and neck, leaving only my face showing as was the custom. I hoped the guards would believe I was a nun arriving to pray with Ruby.

As I backtracked through the servants' corridors and entered the main hallway, I bowed my head to hide my face and slowed to a placid pace to mimic the silent tread of the nuns. My pulse sped with each step, so that by the time I stood in front of the two guards on either side of Ruby's door, I was sure they could hear my thudding heart.

I bowed my head even farther and tucked my hands within the folds of the wide sleeves. "I have come to offer prayers at the request of her Royal Highness."

"We've no knowledge of such a request," said a stocky, giant guard, his voice charged with mistrust.

"She asked for a visit this eve, but the sisters were all detained until now." I held my breath and hoped Ruby was still in the custom of seeking solace from the nuns.

The guards were silent.

Had they recognized my voice? Or had they glimpsed my profile? "You would not deny the princess the only thing she requests, would you?"

The giant guard shifted, his leather boots creaking. "She is already slumbering."

"The child is never too tired for prayer." Though I tried to remain calm, my muscles tightened anyway.

Ruby was angelic, and I was counting on her having won the guards over with her sweet nature so they would do anything for her, even defy the queen.

"Mayhap a short prayer time?" The other guard directed the question to his companion.

"Very well." The giant opened the door and stepped aside. "But be quick."

I glided forward, trying not to seem too eager even as my body hummed with anticipation.

The chamber was dark, the hearth fire banked for the night. But the light from the open doorway aided me as I wove around the maidservants abed on their pallets. The rush mats were still soft, and the herbs within were crushed underfoot so the scents of rosemary and lavender hung in the air.

As I approached the bed, I sensed the guard watching my every movement. I wished I could command him to close the door so I might speak with Ruby privately. But I would have to make the most of the opportunity and hope Ruby cooperated.

Ruby's bed curtains were half-closed, revealing her body underneath the coverlet, a girl on the cusp of womanhood. Upon reaching the bed frame, I kept my head bowed, knelt beside her, and gently laid my hand upon her.

She awoke with a gasp, tensing beneath my touch. Though I refrained from looking at her face, I could feel her relax as she took me in.

"Sister Clare, you have come for prayer?" she asked through a yawn.

I nodded.

She kicked off her coverlet and scooted off the bed. A second later she knelt beside me, folding her hands on the edge of the bed and bowing her head.

I waited several heartbeats. If I startled her with my identity, she'd react too enthusiastically and draw undue attention from the guards. "Our Father," I whispered, leaning closer so my words would carry to her ears and to no one else in the room. I placed my hand over hers and prayed she wouldn't react.

When she remained motionless, I continued. "We thank you for your bountiful protection and that you find ways to reunite sisters."

She stiffened at my strange prayer, but I squeezed her hand, hoping she would understand my urge for caution.

"We beseech you to aid Ruby in being calm so the guards do not discover the true identity of the one kneeling beside her."

Ruby grasped me in return so tightly I was left with no doubt she understood who I was. "Father," she whispered almost inaudibly. "Thank you for preserving my dear sister's life. And now I pray she will leave before it is too late." Ruby squeezed my hand again and then pushed it away, as if sending me the message to go.

Apparently at some point during the past year, Ruby had figured out I wasn't dead. Did she know the queen had tried to murder me? Even if she didn't, she was well aware the queen had evil intentions for me now.

I kept my head low and my tone reverent, but I had to speak directly lest the guards interrupt. "I shall not leave this time unless I have you by my side."

"You must go before she realizes you are here." Ruby's voice turned urgent . . . and too loud.

I brushed my shoulder into hers and reached for her hand again. "We shall go together. I have found a place where we shall be safe—"

"You cannot be here." She lowered her whisper and cast a glance toward the door. "She is using me to draw you here."

I wanted to stand up and drag her from the room, but I forced myself to remain in a prayerful posture. "I saw her edict, and I knew her threat against you was intended to bring me back."

"Then you know you are in grave danger."

"So are you."

She started to shake her head, but I cut off the motion by pressing her hand.

Ruby paused, bowed her head again, and pretended to pray. "I am too young yet to provide a heart for her alchemy. But you are not."

Too young to provide a heart for her alchemy? What was Ruby talking about?

Though I'd never seen the alchemy ingredient list for transforming the white stone, I'd heard of its existence, an ancient sheet tucked away in a compartment in the golden box containing the precious white stone. The language on the sheet was cryptic, and no one had ever been able to decipher it.

Of course, the priests had been trying for years to understand the meaning, and the queen had attempted many experiments. As far as I knew, they'd failed, including the trials using various hearts, mostly of strange, exotic, and dangerous animals.

"Last summer after the Choosing Ball," Ruby continued, her voice barely a whisper, "I overheard Lord Haleigh speaking with the queen about her alchemy."

I pictured the nobleman who had been one of my mother's closest advisors over the years. Father had liked the nobleman and considered him one of the best and wisest of counselors. Lord Haleigh had been a very wealthy man, and he'd had a daughter, a young maiden by the name of Lady Gabriella. At the time I ran away, I'd heard rumors of her unrivaled beauty. Had Lord Haleigh been worried that when Gabriella came of age she might be chosen for the yearly sacrifice to Grendel?

"Lord Haleigh confronted the queen about the death of the fairest maiden." Ruby pressed closer, whispering in my ear. "I heard him say he stumbled upon the priests in the chapel who were removing the heart from the fairest maiden. He accused the queen of using the hearts of the sacrificed maidens every year in her alchemy and said 'tis why the gems in the mountains grow year after year."

If the white stone needed a heart, then it stood to reason that making beautiful gems would require the most beautiful person's heart. Was that why the Choosing Ball singled out the fairest women between eighteen and twenty years? So the queen could gain such a heart for her alchemy?

A sinking weight pressed against my chest. After living on the Great Isle for only a few months, Mikkel had correctly assumed the queen had need of Grendel for her alchemy. How had I not known after all these years? How could I have remained so ignorant?

I wanted to bury my head in frustration and fury.

"Lord Haleigh pleaded with Mother to cease the practice, and if she refused, he threatened to tell the people the truth."

"So she killed him?"

"Yes, how did you know?"

I'd guessed, and it saddened me that my suspicion was right, that I knew our mother well enough to accuse her of murder. Of course she'd want to eliminate anyone who might be a threat to her. "Does Mother know you heard her conversation?"

Ruby hesitated.

The weight inside grew heavier, almost painfully so.

"I did not mean to reveal myself." Ruby's whisper came out in a rush. "But once I heard of her secret ingredient, I believed that was why she killed you, so she could have your heart. I was upset, and the words just came out."

My every thought came to a standstill. All along I'd lamented my mother's attempt to kill me, had wanted to understand what had driven her to do something so despicable. Was this, then, the answer? Had she wanted my heart for her alchemy?

If she needed my heart, why hadn't she waited to take it after the sacrifice to Grendel? Why elaborately plot my murder when she could have obtained what she'd wanted the way she had from maidens for years?

I shook off the questions. Now wasn't the time to dwell on them. What I did understand was that the queen hadn't gotten the heart of the fairest maiden this year as a result of Vilmar's valor, and now she needed mine more than ever. I also understood why she sought Vilmar. He had learned the secret ingredient of her alchemy, and now she needed to silence him. Just as she needed to silence Ruby.

"You must leave with me. The queen will surely kill you for knowing her secrets."

"She has not done so yet."

"If she captures me, she will no longer have any use for you."

"All the more reason for you to be gone and never return."

"I shall not leave without you."

"Please, Pearl. She might keep me as her prisoner, but she will not kill me, not as long as you remain alive."

"Father showed me a secret exit from the castle, one built for use during sieges. That is how I entered, and that is how we shall escape tonight."

Ruby shot a glance toward the soldiers still standing on either side of the open door. "I am not allowed to leave my chambers. Only on rare occasions, and then only under heavy guard."

We had to depart. I'd made it this far, and I couldn't be thwarted. But what kind of excuse could we give the guards? With as much as they seemed to like Ruby, surely they would look the other way if we told them the truth about the danger Ruby was in if she remained anywhere near the queen.

On the other hand, if they allowed Ruby to sneak out of her chambers, the queen would put them to death for negligence. I couldn't abide causing two deaths, not even to save Ruby.

"We have to think of something," I whispered.

"The only way we can survive is for you to stay far away from Mother."

My thoughts continued to swirl, moving faster and growing more desperate, and I lifted a prayer heavenward, one for wisdom and courage.

Ruby reached for my hand, her fingers trembling. I couldn't imagine the heartache and fear she'd lived with over the past year.

There had to be a way to get her away from the guards tonight. Now. Before it grew too late. But what? Could I switch places with her and send her out of the castle in the nun's clothing? We could convince the guards to close the door for a few moments, claiming the need to use the chamber pot, and then exchange garments.

I bit back a sigh. Our bodies were too different. Ruby was stouter like our father, and the guards would recognize that the nun leaving the castle was shorter than the one who'd entered.

At a sudden commotion in the doorway, I stood, determined to grab Ruby and run. But torchlight streamed into Ruby's chamber along with several armed guards.

Ruby rose, and I pushed her behind me with one hand while the other fumbled for the knife hidden in my boot. Before I could slip it free, a woman appeared in the doorway. A beautiful woman with long dark hair, perfect creamy skin, and emerald-green eyes.

Her gaze swept over me, and her lips lifted into a hint of a smile—one that contained no warmth. "Welcome home, Daughter."

Chapter 19

Pearl

"If you spare Ruby and send her away, I shall do whatever you wish."

The queen released a haughty laugh. "You shall do whatever I wish regardless of Ruby."

My knife in hand, I stood taller, braced my feet apart, and lifted my chin. I counted three guards in the room and three more in the hallway, not including the two at the door. I was sorely outnumbered.

Even so, I had to find a way to free Ruby.

The guards held their torches high, illuminating Ruby's few maidservants, who had now arisen from their pallets. They huddled together, their faces reflecting fear. Clearly I could expect no aid from them.

How had the queen discovered my presence? I'd been so quiet and careful. Had one of the knights in the great hall seen me after all and alerted the queen? Though frustration pooled in my chest, I didn't dwell on it. I needed to keep my mind clear and alert so I could devise a new plan. I met the queen's gaze directly, hoping to convey an assurance I didn't feel. "You must allow Ruby to leave. Otherwise, what will the people say when they learn you have murdered both your daughters?"

"They will rejoice to be rid of the threat of treason."

"They will know that one so young as Ruby cannot be involved in treason. And they will despise you for taking her life."

For an instant, uncertainty flickered in the queen's eyes.

"Mother, please." Ruby stepped out from behind me before I could stop her. I attempted to maneuver her back, but she planted her feet and would not be moved. "Please, can we not live together in love and harmony? Is that not more important than wealth and prosperity?"

The queen didn't bother looking at Ruby, almost as if Ruby didn't exist. Instead, she narrowed her eyes upon me. Was she contemplating my warning?

"Send Ruby far away." I had to take advantage of her indecision. "To Scania. I have made friends with Prince Mikkel and will ask him to take Ruby there and assure that she never returns to Warwick."

"So all the princes of Scania have come to the Great Isle for their Testing." The queen watched my face, gauging my reaction.

I kept my expression stoic. I couldn't allow the queen to know just how much I cared about Mikkel. "Send Ruby to Scania with Prince Mikkel. In doing so, you will gain the empathy of the people, and at the same time, you need never worry about her again."

The queen tapped one of her jeweled fingers against her lips. Even at the late hour, she was adorned with gems from the glittering emerald bracelets on her wrists to the sparkling diamonds in her ears. I couldn't remember a time when I'd seen her without her opulent display.

"Very well," the queen replied. "I shall consider your request. But first I should like to meet Prince Mikkel."

So that she could lock him up?

"Invite him to the palace for a banquet."

"There is no need for the trouble. We can send Ruby to him."

"I cannot give him my daughter without assessing his willingness in so great a matter." The queen spoke her lies so smoothly. Had anything she'd ever spoken to me contained truth?

"You need not assess him. He will do this if I but ask."

Even as I fought to keep my feelings for him locked far out of her reach, her eyes narrowed and probed deeply. "We shall hold a banquet on the morrow. And you shall invite him to partake of the feast with us."

I wanted to protest again, but I couldn't, not without eliciting more suspicion. As it was, she had trapped me once more into doing her bidding. The glimmer in her eyes told me she knew it.

My only option for saving Ruby was to invite Mikkel into her clutches. The queen wouldn't set me free—not if she needed my heart. But I would pray Mikkel's offer of an alliance with Scania would satisfy her enough to allow him and Ruby their freedom.

And if she detained him with the hope of drawing

Vilmar out of hiding? She might be able to confine him a short while, but she would have to set him free erelong.

Truly, I had no concern over what became of me, as long as Ruby and Mikkel were safe.

As if sensing my conclusion, the queen waved a hand at one of her guards. "Take Princess Pearl to her chambers. Once she has written an invitation to Prince Mikkel, bring it to me so I might also add a personal note. We want him to know he is indeed most welcome here in Warwick."

I didn't resist as the guards drew up alongside me and took my knife. Before they could usher me away, I pressed a hand against Ruby's cheek, silently imploring her to remain strong no matter what the future held.

She placed her hand over mine, her eyes assuring me we would get through this together. She'd grown taller over the year I'd been gone. At twelve years of age she was almost my height—and almost as brave.

The queen spun and glided from the room, pausing in the doorway. "See that the servants draw a bath for Princess Pearl and make her as beautiful as possible for the feast." She smiled at me over her shoulder. "After all, why not give the prince more incentive to do as you request?"

My stomach rolled with growing unease. Did the queen think she could use my beauty to manipulate Mikkel? Had she guessed we had a relationship that went beyond friendship? What she didn't know was that Mikkel would feel betrayed and hurt when he realized I'd been lying to him about my deformities. It would diminish his feelings for me, not increase them.

As the queen exited into the hallway, I allowed my

shoulders to slump with despair. I prayed that after such betrayal, Mikkel would still be willing to take Ruby with him to Scania.

MIKKEL

Gregor and I searched the city throughout the night, questioning everyone we met about whether they knew of another way into the castle, perhaps a secret passageway. The architects had surely planned for a second entrance and exit, knowing that having only one so high up the mountain might prove deadly during a siege.

If there was another way inside, no one knew of it. Growing weary and frustrated, we returned to the tavern at the first hint of dawn, ready to quench our thirst and sate our hunger before we climbed up to the gatehouse and waited for it to open.

As soon as we stepped into the dim interior, I sensed the change in atmosphere from the proprietor and other patrons who were already awake. Gone was the friendliness. Instead, hostility spiked the air, and I sensed we were no longer welcome there.

The tavern owner handed me a rolled-up parchment. "This came for you while you were gone."

As I took it, I followed his gaze to a deep-red wax seal. It bore the imprint of two lions standing rampant, forelegs raised, ready to strike.

"From the queen herself." His voice was accusatory.

How had the queen discovered our presence here at

the tavern? Had someone we talked to during the night notified her of our questions? Worse, had she forced Pearl to tell her?

My gut churned at the prospect that Pearl's mission had failed. Though I wasn't pleased she'd gone into the castle on her own, I'd held out hope that her plan to kidnap Ruby would prevail. After all, Pearl was intelligent, quick-thinking, and capable. If anyone could achieve the daring feat, she could.

"When did this come?" I asked.

The proprietor glared at me. "A few hours ago. Soldiers came for Prince Mikkel."

I didn't confirm or deny the man's silent question about my identity. Instead, I slid my finger into the seal and broke it. Unrolling the missive, the first thing I noticed was Pearl's signature near the bottom.

My worst fears had been realized. The queen had captured Pearl.

I wanted to slam my fist into something but forced myself to remain calm. I scanned the sheet, all the while aware that every pair of eyes in the room was upon me, gauging my reaction.

"You are officially invited to attend a banquet in the royal palace. Her Royal Highness, Queen Margery, requests the opportunity to meet you before giving Ruby over to your guardianship."

Pearl's note was impersonal, almost cold, with an invitation from the queen at the bottom. It was obvious the queen was manipulating Pearl into doing her bidding, no doubt using Ruby as leverage. It was also obvious Pearl had bargained with the queen so she would release Ruby to me. Likely she'd offered her own life to save Ruby's.

Protest burned in my chest.

The tavern owner cleared his throat, but once again I refused to acknowledge him. This wasn't his business, and the less he knew about it, the safer he'd be.

I'd attend the feast, but I wasn't leaving with just Ruby. I'd make my offer of an alliance with Scania, but with the stipulation that the queen release Pearl to me as well. Of course I wanted to help Ruby escape to safety. But I wanted to save Pearl more than anything.

The simple truth was that I loved her.

I sank to the nearest bench, the revelation too overwhelming and the prospect of losing her too staggering. Somehow over the past weeks, I'd fallen in love with Princess Pearl.

It didn't matter anymore what was beneath her veil. Even if she was scarred worse than Gregor, I still loved her. I loved her for who she was and not for how she looked. Wasn't that what I'd been learning in my Testing—not just to accept people who were different but to actually love and cherish them for their uniqueness?

I sat up taller, straightening my spine and resolving to love and cherish Pearl as long as we both lived. She was worth more than a country. She was worth more than a kingship. She was worth more than my own life. She was priceless. And I'd do anything for her.

"I shall need a bath and clean garments." I directed my request to Gregor. "Come what may, I must dine with the queen and shall present myself to her as favorably as possible. If I am to negotiate for the release of Princess Pearl and Princess Ruby, I shall need every advantage."

All I had at my disposal was negotiation. I would have to work hard to bargain with the queen and pray she would accept.

Chapter 20

As the double doors of the great hall swung open, I straightened the royal-blue tunic along with the fashionable breeches and hose Gregor had managed to find. I didn't ask him how he tracked down the garments, but he had likely gained the cooperation of the tavern owner.

Gregor had assisted me with bathing and shaving as well as trimming my hair. When finished, he plaited one thin strand on the side and left the rest unbound. For the first time since sailing away from Scania, I had the appearance befitting a prince.

During a moment of wishing for a mirror to examine myself, I'd realized how much I always relied upon my appearance for confidence. As part of my Testing, not only had I needed to see past the appearances of others, but I'd needed to see deeper into my own motives. In comparing myself to Vilmar for so many years, I'd tried to compensate by making myself look better. Now it was past time to accept our differences, and in particular, accept myself.

Even though I was no longer on the Isle of Outcasts with my official Testing, I could still continue to grow no matter where I was or what challenges I faced. In fact, perhaps that was the true Testing—to mature my entire life in every circumstance and to accept that even kings weren't exempt from growth, especially kings who hoped to do great things for their people.

Whatever the case, I had to present myself to Queen Margery with the bearing of a king. To do any less with this crafty woman would diminish my chances of securing Pearl and Ruby.

Squaring my shoulders, I started through the doors and into the great hall. The room was teeming with guests, and at my appearance, the murmur of their voices faded, leaving only the soft strum of a harp. I strode forward regardless of the attention upon me, infusing each step with determination and purpose.

Drawing near the dais, I scanned faces, finding Gregor's in the shadows of the kitchen hallway where he'd told me he'd wait. Pearl wasn't amongst the nobility. Instead, the queen sat upon her throne, watching my approach with undisguised interest.

As I regarded the queen in return, I had to stifle my surprise at how beautiful she was. Although I'd only seen Pearl's face above her veil, it was obvious she'd inherited her mother's beauty. They shared the same elegant features, same lustrous raven hair, and same mesmerizing green eyes.

I stopped at the bottom step of the dais and waited for Lord Anise, the nobleman who'd served as my companion since entering the castle, to now present me to the queen.

"Your Royal Majesty." Lord Anise stepped out from

behind me and bowed low to the queen. Perhaps in the past I might have been impressed by a young man like him—handsome, witty, and clearly having earned the queen's favor. But after months of living with the outcasts, I saw past his outer demeanor and recognized him as someone who was looking for advancement at court by any means possible. Men like him weren't trustworthy and could easily switch loyalties depending on what they could gain.

He rose and then bowed toward me, although not as fully. "May I present Prince Mikkel Holberg, son of King Christian of the great kingdom of Scania."

I refused to kneel before this queen. Doing so would feed her appetite for power, and I couldn't allow her to believe even for a moment that I was weak in any way. Instead, I dipped my head in the greeting between equals.

She held out her hand. Each finger contained multiple rings with varying jewels, and her wrists, numerous bracelets of emeralds, rubies, sapphires, and diamonds. She was obviously putting her wealth on display—or at least what she had left of it.

I couldn't ignore her as I wanted to do, but I waited several seconds longer before I took her hand and pressed the barest of kisses there. As I straightened, her gaze was cool, as though she recognized my slight toward her authority.

"Your Majesty, thank you for the invitation." I infused as much coolness into my tone as possible.

"Princess Pearl insisted."

That was a lie. Pearl hadn't wanted me to come near the queen, had wanted to protect me from the same ill will that had befallen Vilmar. But if the queen wanted to play this game of deception, I would allow it.

"I could not deny her," the queen continued, "especially when she indicated you are willing to provide sanctuary to Princess Ruby."

"Scania is willing to provide sanctuary to both princesses. After all, they are family." Since my mother was related to Queen Margery, Pearl and Ruby were my distant cousins, though family ties had nothing to do with why I wanted them to live in Scania.

"You are gracious to make such a generous offer. However, since both colluded in plotting treason, I must hold at least one of them accountable. Do you not agree?"

The queen's attention flickered to a side room. Was that where she was holding Pearl? I had the urge to run over, throw open the door, and set Pearl free. But I held myself back. I had to use caution, or I'd cause more trouble for all of us.

"I know nothing about treason," I answered. "But Princess Pearl has assured me of her desire to leave Warwick. She will nevermore consider returning and will live out the rest of her days in Scania."

The queen's keen eyes remained upon me as though trying to read my mind. "Princess Pearl is beguiling, is she not, Your Highness? Surely you can agree a beauty such as hers has the power to influence a man, even one as strong as you."

I had to answer carefully lest I fall into one of the queen's traps—one of the many she was setting for me with each sentence she spoke. "Princess Pearl is indeed beautiful. But she has proven her true power to influence comes from within."

The queen sat back against her throne, a smile playing upon her lips. "She has already beguiled you."

I shook my head. "No—"

"I see it in your eyes. You care about her. Dare I say you even love her and wish to take her back to Scania to be your wife?"

A part of me wanted to tell the queen the truth, that Pearl was already my wife. But would the queen be more agreeable to my bargaining if she felt as though she had more to give in exchange for an alliance, especially if she could offer Pearl as my bride?

I needed to force her hand now, in front of her court. Then we would have witnesses to whatever agreement we might reach. "I am prepared to provide you an alliance with Scania in exchange for both princesses."

"You are but a prince and have no authority to make such a decision."

"I shall be king."

The queen smiled, but her lips were thin and her eyes cold. "What about Prince Vilmar? What if he becomes king instead of you?"

Something in the way the queen spoke baited me, almost as if she hoped I would be willing to work against Vilmar to eliminate my competition for the throne. I kept my expression neutral, unwilling to reveal that the bond with my brother went beyond our Testing and that I would never betray him.

"Vilmar may be charming." I chose my words with care. "But he isn't cunning enough to become king."

The queen watched me, waiting for me to continue.

"I shall become king, and therefore you would do well to remain in my favor, especially because an alliance with Scania would be of great benefit to your country."

She tapped her lips with one finger. "Perhaps."

Before I could say more, she stood, and several servants rushed to aid her. She started toward the table that was already set with fine linens, crystal goblets, and silver dishes. Kitchen servants hovered in a nearby hallway holding platters and jugs. The waft of mutton and other roasted meats hung in the air.

I hadn't partaken in a grand meal since the one in honor of our commissioning for our Testing the night before we left Scania. But I had no appetite for one today, not unless I could guarantee Pearl's safety.

"I'm sure you are already well aware of the benefits of forming an alliance with Scania." I could list them, but I didn't want her to believe I was desperate—even though I was.

She paused near her chair at the center of the table. "Yes, but your father already spurned me, did not think Warwick was good enough for him."

"I am not my father."

"Then you love Princess Pearl?" She pinned me with a gaze that wouldn't allow me to deny it. And why should I, when admitting it could seal the bargain?

"Yes. I love her."

Chapter 21

Pearl

Mikkel loved me?

I sagged against the buttery door.

He loved me. The prospect was too great to comprehend, and I could only stare at the crack of light coming from underneath the door, illuminating the darkness.

He still believed I was blemished. He'd never seen me without my veil. For all he knew, I was unbearably ugly underneath. And yet, he loved me regardless.

Warmth blossomed deep inside, and I couldn't contain a smile. Though the circumstances were appalling and my body was still trembling with fear at what the queen would do to Mikkel, the realization that he loved me so unconditionally awoke in me a sense of belonging. Belonging together.

Though I'd clung to the notion of annulling our marriage someday, I knew now I never would have been able to make myself go through with it. Not when we belonged so perfectly to each other.

"So you think that by bringing Princess Pearl to Scania and marrying her you will forge an alliance with Warwick?" The queen's voice was much too calculated.

Mikkel was silent for a long moment. Would he reveal that we were already married? I wasn't sure that doing so would aid his cause in rescuing me. In fact, I suspected nothing would, not when the queen needed my heart for her alchemy.

I leaned against the door again and bowed my head. What had I expected now that I knew the truth about his love? That Mikkel and I would be able to live happily ever after together? Such endings only happened in fairy tales.

"Having Warwick's princesses in Scania would give my country more reason to contribute to Warwick's successes."

"You have given me much to ponder, Prince Mikkel. I shall discuss the matter with my advisors and then decide. For now, let us enjoy the feast."

The harp music began again along with the clinking of goblets and dishes.

I could only pray the queen would agree to Mikkel's proposal of an alliance. But even if she did so here in front of her court so publicly, she was not as principled as Mikkel. While he was a man of his word and would follow through with a vow, the queen would think nothing of changing her mind. If she wanted my heart, she would find a way to get it, no matter what promises she made to Mikkel.

I brushed my hand against the layers of my best ruby gown studded with diamonds at my waist and all throughout the bodice. The servants had spent hours bathing and grooming me, fawning over every detail of my appearance, knowing that the queen would expect nothing less than perfection. They'd taken extra care with my hair, styling it with a few strands pulled up in order to show off my diamond earrings and necklace as well as a tiara of rubies and diamonds.

Why had the queen gone to so much trouble with my appearance? If she hoped to show me to the people as a traitor and rebel, why not leave me in my tattered travel garments?

I started to slide down to the floor, but at the rattle of the key in the lock, I straightened. Was the queen sending me back to my chambers? Would she kill me there while everyone feasted? While she distracted Mikkel?

I pressed my hands together, wishing I had my knife to defend myself, for I doubted this time I'd be so fortunate as to have a servant rise up to free me as the huntsman had done the last time the queen tried to have me murdered.

The door opened to reveal Lord Anise, one of Mother's favorite young noblemen. "Your Highness," he said with a bow. "The queen requests your presence at the banquet."

"How kind of her." While I might not understand her scheming, I did know she was never without an ulterior motive.

Lord Anise motioned for me to move ahead of him out the door and down the short passageway. As I stepped into the full light of the sconces, his eyes widened at the sight of me in all my glittering jewels.

"You look beautiful, Your Highness," he said almost reverently.

I nodded but pressed my lips together. Perhaps the queen intended to show the people I was regal and grown up enough to be a contender for the throne. Would seeing me in such glory prove that her claims of my treason were true?

As I stepped through the arched doorway into the great hall, I was suddenly overcome with trepidation. Mikkel would see me without my veil for the first time.

Attention shifted to me and the conversation within the great hall lessened until only a few people were talking. I stared around the room, everywhere but at Mikkel. When I reached the few steps that led to the head table, I finally allowed myself to seek him out.

He was the handsomest man there. He'd taken care with his appearance, leaving his fair hair long and loose with a narrow plait that gave him a slightly rugged look. Although he'd shaven, he couldn't dispense altogether with his scruffiness.

In conversation with a nobleman seated next to him, he hadn't noticed me yet. When the nobleman glanced at me and ceased speaking midsentence, Mikkel gave me a cursory look, then reached for his goblet. He froze midway there, and his attention returned to me.

His eyes rounded, revealing beautiful silvery-blue mingled with awe. He jumped to his feet so quickly his chair toppled backward.

"Lords and ladies," Lord Anise spoke from beside me. "I present to you Her Royal Highness, Princess Pearl."

Across the room, benches scraped as people rose. They bowed and curtsied, but none of their expressions welcomed me. No one dared to show even the slightest happiness at seeing me, not when I was so despised by the queen.

I caught Mikkel's gaze again, hoping for at least one friendly face amongst the crowd. But his brow had furrowed. The awe was gone, and instead his eyes sparked with anger.

Of course he wasn't glad to see the real me after all this time. Not after I'd lied to him about what was beneath my veil.

As I reached the top step, he seemed to force himself into action, stalking toward me. I halted and waited for him to finish approaching, his footsteps echoing an ominous rhythm.

"Your Highness." He bowed and then held out his arm.

"Your Highness." I took his proffer, tucking my fingers into the crook of his elbow, trying not to let them shake.

He led me behind the table. "I trust you are well."

"Yes, as well as can be."

"I'm glad you are able to join the feast."

Was he? He was looking straight ahead, his jaw flexing, his expression still unyielding.

I wished for a private moment to speak with him, but the queen must have orchestrated our first meeting in this public place so we would have no opportunity to confer with one another. What should I say? Should I apologize?

"I am heartily sorry," I whispered.

He didn't reply and instead pulled out my chair, standing aloof, waiting for me to sit before he pushed me in and took his place beside me.

As conversation began to resume around the great

hall, I reached for my goblet and leaned closer to him. "Forgive me, Mikkel. Please."

He stabbed his knife into a wedge of mutton and dropped the meat onto his trencher. "You deceived me."

"I had to in the camp for the same reason you had to hide your identity. Everyone would have shunned me and sent me away."

"You could have told me," he hissed. "I would have kept your secret."

I nodded and fiddled with the spoon next to my trencher, aware that almost everyone was still staring at me. I'd been accustomed to such attention growing up, but after the past year of living behind my veil and in seclusion on the island, the stares felt invasive.

"I understand that you may not have trusted me initially." He stabbed another piece of mutton. "But in recent days, I thought I'd proven my loyalty to you."

All my excuses for not telling him the truth now seemed flimsy and irrelevant, for he had proven himself many times over.

He lifted the mutton, sank his teeth into it, and ripped off a juicy bite. With his broad shoulders hunched, he stared straight ahead while he chewed.

"It does not matter anymore," I whispered. "She will kill me for my heart, and you can do naught to stop her."

He paused in taking another bite to glare at me.

"Please, I beg you to take Ruby and go while you still can."

"Princess Pearl." The queen's voice sliced through our whispered conversation.

I sat up straighter and peered at the queen several

places away. She was attired in one of her loveliest gowns—a dark green that brought out the green in her eyes. Like most of her garments, this one contained intricate jewels throughout, making her glitter.

"Enlighten me." She toyed with her goblet, running her finger around the rim. "Prince Mikkel has declared his love for you. Do you feel the same about him?"

I probably loved him more. But I couldn't say so. If I did, she'd use Mikkel to make me submit to her every whim. He would be safer if I severed my connection to him now while I still could.

"No." I kept my attention on the queen and didn't let it stray to Mikkel. I didn't want to see the hurt my words were sure to cause him. "No, I do not love the prince, and I shall not go to Scania with him."

Chapter 22

I tried to finish swallowing the piece of meat, but it stuck in my throat. Maybe my feelings were stronger than hers for me. Maybe she didn't love me yet. But I hadn't imagined the attraction that had grown between us, and I knew she liked me.

I dropped my knife and the rest of the mutton to my trencher and swished my fingers in the pewter washing bowl at my place setting. I rinsed them of grease and food, my appetite washing away just as easily. All the while, I studied Pearl's face, really taking her in for the first time.

Her cheeks were high boned and elegant, her nose a perfect shape, her lips alluring, and her chin delicately rounded. Her flawless creamy skin contrasted with her dark unbound hair cascading in long curls.

Not only was her face breathtakingly beautiful, but her body was too. I'd only seen her in loose-fitting men's tunics and breeches. And now, her red gown highlighted an alluring womanly form.

Altogether, she was remarkably stunning. What word had the queen used? Beguiling?

I understood why the queen believed Pearl's beauty had cast a spell over me, making me fall in love with her. Even now, I could see the way Lord Anise and the other young noblemen regarded her with admiration.

Was it possible the queen was jealous of her daughter? Perhaps she didn't like sharing the attention. Or perhaps she feared Pearl would win over the favor of the citizens. For the queen lacked the one thing Pearl possessed: inner beauty. Pearl's compassion, benevolence, and solicitude toward others would make her the better queen by far.

Though I didn't like that Pearl had deceived me about what was behind the veil, I could understand the wisdom of her plan. Knowing the man I'd once been before my Testing, a man who'd valued appearances, I would have focused on her outward beauty and missed the incredible woman she was on the inside.

The fact was, I'd fallen in love with her for who she was and not for what she looked like. And I wasn't sure that would have happened without the veil.

I dried my hands on my garments, then shifted in my chair so I was face-to-face with her. "I forgive you," I whispered.

Her long lashes lifted, framing her expressive eyes— eyes I'd grown to love as windows into her soul. And now they filled with both surprise and tenderness. "I am truly sorry. I should have told you sooner—"

I covered her lips with mine, pressing in and claiming her. She was mine. I loved her. And I wanted her to know that no matter what might happen, no matter how much she denied loving me in return, I would never stop loving her.

Her lashes fell, but not before I caught sight of the pleasure in her eyes. And when she arched to meet me, her lips melding against mine with passion, I knew she loved me too, that she'd denied it to protect me.

I didn't care that every person in the room, including the queen, was watching us. I didn't care that peril lurked at every move. I loved Pearl more than I'd ever believed possible, and I wanted her to know that.

"Very nice." The queen's voice cut into me, and I backed away at the same time Pearl broke our kiss. "The two of you have indeed enlightened me just as I'd hoped you would."

Her tone contained a hint of threat, one that told me she was playing a deadly game. But even with the queen looking on, I couldn't tear my attention from Pearl, from her full, rounded lips, from the way she pressed those lips together to resemble a delectable pucker, one that beckoned me to bend in and kiss her again and never stop.

As though sensing the direction of my thoughts, Pearl shifted, letting her hair fall like a veil, blocking her face from my view.

I blinked, then gave myself a mental shake, trying to force myself to think of something else besides Pearl and how much I wanted to draw her into my arms and hold her. Was this the battle I would have fought if she'd revealed herself to me earlier? Focusing too much on the physical attraction to the detriment of everything else?

I could feel the queen's gaze still upon us. Perhaps in showing my love for Pearl, I could prove I had no other motive for requesting Pearl's freedom.

I brushed the curtain of hair away from Pearl's face, giving myself full view of her profile, the delicate lines of her face, and her unguarded beauty. I bent in and brushed a kiss against her cheek.

"Mikkel, behave." She leaned away, a soft blush infusing her face.

"Very well. If you insist." I sat up, straightened my shoulders, and pretended to be occupied by my food. From the corner of my eye, I caught her watching me, a slight smile upon her lips. In that moment I realized I hadn't seen her smile yet. There had been few reasons to smile. And even if she had, I wouldn't have been able to observe it behind her veil.

What could I do to make her smile? Really smile?

The usual compliments regarding her appearance wouldn't mean anything to her. In fact, she probably tired easily of such flattery. And I wasn't a charmer anyway.

If we'd been in Scania, I would have lavished upon her gifts of every variety and size. Or I would have taken her somewhere special or done something to show her how much I cared. But here, now, I had only myself to give.

I slid my hand underneath the table and reached for hers. At my touch, she startled and began to pull away. I intertwined my fingers with hers, capturing her and drawing her closer. "I meant what I said."

"And what was that?"

I rested our hands on my thigh and stroked my thumb over hers.

She didn't make a move to pull away, but the flush returned to her cheeks.

"I love you, Pearl."

Her rounded eyes met mine. Uncertainty lingered in the green depths.

"What will it take for me to convince you of my sincerity?"

"You need not convince me. I believe you."

"You do?"

She nodded and then glanced at the queen. "But 'tis unwise to speak of love."

"She saw my love for you even before I spoke of it. I cannot hide how I feel for you, not even if I tried my hardest."

She studied my face as though memorizing me. The longing and love in her eyes spoke louder than words. I lifted her hand to my lips and kissed her knuckles. "I shall always love you," I whispered before kissing her hand again.

As she watched my gentle kiss, her lips parted and she sucked in a short breath. The soft sound sparked a low flame inside me so that I could think of nothing else but kissing her lips once more. I swooped in and took another kiss before she could protest, giving in to the fullness and sweetness of her mouth, savoring her and yet not sated.

She pulled away with a soft laugh. "Mikkel, you must stop. Everyone is staring."

"I don't care."

Leaning in, I intended to show her how little regard I had for the queen and her courtiers. But she pressed a piece of cheese into my mouth. Apparently, I amused her, for she laughed once more.

I loved hearing her laughter and would let her ply me with food all day long if I could hear more of it. I chewed and swallowed and allowed her to feed me again while picking up cheese and doing the same to her.

When we finished the final course, Queen Margery rose from her chair. Immediately, the guests stood, even those at the head table. All except me. Pearl tugged my hand still intertwined with hers. Only then did I push away from the table, but slowly. No matter how desperate the circumstances, I was still a prince of Scania and would act like the future king.

The queen beckoned to a side doorway to soldiers who'd congregated there. As they filed into the room and made their way to the dais, uneasiness prodded me. The queen wouldn't call her knights to surround us if she planned to let Pearl accompany me to Scania. In fact, it was becoming clear that she'd anticipated my bargain for Pearl and had brought in her soldiers to ensure I wouldn't try to take Pearl by force.

"During the course of the feast," the queen said, "everyone has witnessed the truth."

The clanking footsteps of the soldiers echoed in the great hall, highlighting the silence.

"The truth is that the prince of Scania is conspiring with Princess Pearl—"

"Conspiring?" I gripped the hilt of my sword, offended by so harsh an accusation. "That isn't true."

"You intend to marry her and then stir the simpleminded of this country to fight against me and support you."

"I have a country of my own and have no need of another—"

"You have no guarantee of kingship, and therefore seek to take mine with Princess Pearl by your side, rallying the people of this country."

The queen knew I didn't aspire to her throne any more than Pearl did. The accusation was her attempt to conceal more sinister deeds. But what? "I have offered Warwick a partnership with Scania in exchange for the life of the woman I love and her younger sister. That is the extent of my designs."

"Yes, we have certainly all witnessed the way you are

taken with my daughter. And because of your feelings for her, she will be able to persuade you to do anything she wishes, including usurping Warwick's throne."

"I have no wish for Warwick's throne. Now or ever."

"But the princess does, and you have proven your loyalty lies with her."

"We shall leave for Scania this very day. Your men may even accompany us to assure our departure."

One of the queen's narrow brows rose. "You know as well as I do that many queens and kings have continued to plot treason when they are banished afar. If I allow her to live in Scania, what is to prevent her from charming you into doing whatever she asks, including using Scania's resources and army to plot against me?"

"If I allow her to live." The words reverberated through me, rattling my bones and sending fear along my nerves. Even though the queen had tried to murder Pearl once before, how had she so easily condemned Pearl to death without a trial and without any recourse?

The knights drew closer and surrounded Pearl and me. Surely the queen had no plans to arrest me along with Pearl. She wouldn't dare, would she?

The fear in Pearl's eyes told me the queen would dare.

A part of me was tempted to call Gregor to my aid, but I sensed I was still undergoing my Testing, that even if I wasn't on the Isle of Outcasts any longer, these current challenges were still a part of shaping me.

No, I wouldn't rely upon Gregor to help get me out of the situation. I had to do this for myself or die trying. That was the way of honor.

"I beseech you once again to consider my offer of an alliance," I said to the queen. "And if you pay it no heed, then I ask that you take me as your prisoner instead of Princess Pearl. Allow my manservant to take her to Scania with Ruby, and I shall remain your prisoner for as long as I live."

"No!" Pearl stepped toward me only to have the guards cut her off, hemming her in even closer. "I shall not allow you to suffer on my behalf."

Her voice was infused with stubbornness. But at this moment, I refused to allow her to have her way. I had to get her out of Warwick and away from the queen. And if that meant I had to sacrifice myself to win her freedom, then so be it. Perhaps later, I'd be able to negotiate with the queen further for my own release. But even if she kept me forever, I had to save Pearl.

"Let Mikkel go!" Pearl pushed against the knights. "'Tis me you want! You need my heart, not his."

Heart? She'd mentioned the queen wanting her heart before. What did she mean by it? Surely not her physical heart, the one that pumped lifeblood throughout her body. But what if that's exactly what the queen wanted. Why would she need it?

I didn't have time to process this revelation. Instead I held out my arms to the closest knights. "Take me."

"This is altogether too touching." The queen's expression was rigid and cold upon Pearl. "But you may as well hold your tongues, for I have no intention of setting either one of you free. I intend to behead you both. For treason."

Pearl screamed. I shoved against the soldiers who'd taken hold of me, unsheathing my knife and rapidly slicing into the closest knights. But a dozen more converged upon me. I was outnumbered, and though I fought valiantly, they subdued me, wresting the weapon from my grip and divesting me of the rest. Within seconds, I was chained and being pushed from the room, with Pearl's cries echoing around me.

Chapter 23

Pearl

I pounded against the chamber door, but my efforts had grown weak, my hand bruised, and my body trembled from grief. I sagged against the heavy oaken panel, pressing my tear-streaked cheek to the cold wood.

I was locked inside with no way to escape. I'd attempted every possible means, from trying to pry open the window to pulling up floorboards in hopes of finding a secret tunnel. But after nearly two days, I'd concluded that the only way out was through the door.

But the door wouldn't budge no matter how much I tugged on it, and I hadn't been able to bang it down with my bare hands either.

"Oh, Mikkel." More tears slipped out. "Why did you have to come here with me? Why didn't you stay back on the island?"

The words I'd once spoken to Mikkel came back to me: *"True love makes one do things one would not normally consider."* Perhaps he'd left the island because he'd loved and accepted me even then, long before his declaration.

I pushed away from the door and paced across the rushes to my bed, then spun on my heel and circled back to the door. "You were a fool to think you could come here and reason with the queen. No one can ever reason with her. Not my father, not her closest advisors, and not even me. Especially not me."

Why did she hate me? Why? I was her daughter. The question that had taunted me for so long now swelled and threatened to choke me.

"I hate you too!" The tears ran down my cheeks faster. "Hate you, hate you, hate you!"

I beat my fists against the door again, letting my anger surface and add strength to my hatred. If I ever saw her again, I'd take her by surprise and plunge a knife into her heart. If I couldn't find a knife, I'd strangle her with my bare hands.

The moment I pictured myself squeezing the sensitive spot in her throat, I gasped with sudden horror. What was I doing? What was I thinking? How could I even contemplate killing her?

I'd vowed not to allow myself to become the same kind of monster as the queen, a monster who cared so little for her family that she'd kill them. But here I was. Plotting how I would take my mother's life the next time I was with her.

With a groan, I crumpled into a heap and buried my face in my hands, my ruby-colored dress pooling around me. The queen had sent my servants away. But even if they'd been allowed to attend me, I wouldn't have bothered to change out of the gown. I hadn't cared what I wore after hearing my mother's declaration to behead Mikkel. All I'd done was lament and foster my hatred toward my mother, and now it had led me to contemplate murder.

"What have I done?" I groaned again. "What have I become?"

At a soft rapping against the door, I sat up and swiped the moisture from my cheeks.

"Pearl?" Ruby's muffled voice came from the other side.

I scrambled to my feet.

"Mother said I could visit you in order to say farewell."

I watched the door. The second the guards opened it, I intended to push my way out, locate Mikkel, and set him free.

Ruby spoke again. "She warned that if you attempt anything at all, she'll make Mikkel suffer rather than ending his life quickly."

My legs gave way, and I collapsed to the floor again. A sob rose in my chest, but I swallowed hard in order to push my despair down.

The door opened a crack, and Ruby's face peeked through. A moment later, she slipped inside and the door closed behind her firmly, letting me know that while Ruby might be able to come in, I wouldn't be allowed out. Not that I'd attempt an escape now, not with the queen's threat against Mikkel.

Ruby dropped to her knees and grabbed me in a hug. I tossed my arms around her too. We clung to each other, and even when she wiggled to free herself, I was unwilling to let go, since this might be the last time I'd get to see her.

"Please, Pearl," she whispered. "I have much to say

and not enough time."

Reluctantly, I released her. "Then she is planning to execute me soon?"

Ruby pressed a finger to her lips. Then cocking her head to the opposite side of the room, she dragged me up and tugged me away from the door.

"She has sent out the announcement for your beheading," Ruby whispered, "to take place on this afternoon. But she has not established a day yet for Mikkel's execution."

"Good. Maybe it is only a ruse to draw in Vilmar. Maybe once she has my heart, she will release Mikkel."

"If I have my way, we shall not give her anything."

"I deserve to die, Ruby." We stopped at the bed, and I lowered myself to the edge.

"No, you do not—"

"I have become a monster just like her." My head and shoulders drooped under my shame.

Ruby sat beside me and held my hands. "'Tis true that you have many of her qualities. You are beautiful and strong and intelligent. But you are not a monster. Not even close."

"I am close. Closer than you realize."

"I know you, and you care about people, truly care. And Mother has never loved anyone but herself."

Ruby was right. Mother had never loved anyone, not even Father. Perhaps she'd harbored some affection for him, but never the self-sacrificing love he'd shown toward her.

"You are different than her, Pearl."

"I wanted to kill her."

"I have too."

I lifted my head to study her face. "Really?"

"After I overheard her conversation with Lord Haleigh and understood what she was doing with the hearts of the young maidens, I wanted to get rid of her." Ruby's eyes reflected the same despair swirling through me. And loss.

We'd both lost hope in ever having what we longed for—a mother who loved us. It was only right to grieve and mourn. But Ruby hadn't let her despair turn into bitterness or hatred. Perhaps that's where I'd gone amiss. Maybe that's where our mother had gone amiss, too, so long ago. She'd fostered bitterness toward her family, which led to hatred. And eventually, that hatred had controlled her until she was incapable of loving.

I couldn't allow that to happen. I couldn't give bitterness a home inside me. I had to evict it. But how? I couldn't change my disappointment in my mother for not loving Ruby and me the way we'd needed, but I could find a way to move on from it, couldn't I?

As if sensing my questions, Ruby made the sign of the cross on her shoulders and chest. "Whenever I confessed my murderous hatred to Sister Clare, she quoted the Holy Scripture that says: *'When ye stand praying, forgive, if ye have ought against any: that your Father also which is in heaven may forgive you your trespasses.'"*

If I wanted God to forgive me for my wicked thoughts of murdering my mother, then I needed to forgive her?

"'Bitterness leads to bondage, but forgiveness sets us free,'" Ruby continued. "That's what Sister Clare always says."

I didn't understand how forgiveness could set me

free, but before I could voice my question, a commanding voice came from the other side of the doorway.

Ruby's grip on my hands tightened. "Listen to me. During the march to the bailey green, Gregor and a few of your friends from the Isle of Outcasts will create a diversion so you can escape."

My pulse gave a sudden lurch. "My friends from the island are here?"

"I don't know who." Her whisper was impatient. "I only know what Gregor's message revealed."

I marveled that any of the outcasts had left the safety of the island to come to Warwick. That meant they'd departed shortly after we had. Had they sensed the danger we would face? Why would they take such a risk by following?

A tiny thrill tingled inside, the first hope I'd had since my mother had captured me. "What about Mikkel? How are they planning to free him?"

"Gregor did not speak of it, only that you must get away as soon as the attack begins."

My thoughts traveled back to the evening in Fife at sunset when we'd rescued Felicity and the other two women. Together we'd schemed, but Mikkel's ingenuity and ideas had helped us prevail.

At the tap against the door and the soldier calling Ruby's name, she stood, and all my fears came rushing back.

The royal mountaintop fortress was nothing like the small fishing town of Fife. The queen was much more capable than the Inquisitor. And the elite guards in the palace made the soldiers in Fife look like children in comparison. An escape would be nearly impossible through the gatehouse. And even more challenging through the secret tunnel.

How would Gregor or any one of my outcast friends survive the confrontation, much less make it out of the fortress undetected and alive?

As the door handle rattled, Ruby stood. "Promise you will do everything within your power to escape?"

"If you are with me."

She hesitated.

"The queen will likely force you to be on the green to watch me die. Once the commotion starts, you must run away with me."

"I shall only slow you down."

"No. We go together or not at all."

She pursed her lips. As the door opened, she nodded. "Very well. I shall try."

"Good."

"One last thing," she whispered. "I heard the queen talking about how she didn't need the jewels anymore since she'd soon have gold. What could she mean?"

A soldier stepped into the room, his weapons drawn, his expression severe as he glanced from Ruby to me and back. "Time is up, Your Highness."

Ruby sniffled and pretended to cry before she threw her arms around me.

It was the giant guard who'd stood outside Ruby's door the night I'd snuck in. The guard had the grace to look chagrined. Staring at the floor, he waited, clearly liking Ruby and feeling sorry for her. I could only hope that favor would continue once we attempted to escape from the castle later.

Ruby pressed a kiss against my cheek. "What if Mother wants your heart because she believes it will aid the white stone in creating gold?"

She didn't give me the chance to answer. Instead, she released me and started toward the guard, sniffling again and brushing at her cheeks. After she was gone, I stared at the closed door, her question rattling in my head and growing louder with each passing second.

The queen had established the requirements for the Choosing Ball because she needed a specific heart to mix with the white stone for her alchemy. A heart belonging to the most beautiful maiden in the land, a maiden not younger than eighteen but no older than twenty.

If such a heart was necessary to produce precious gems, then what kind of heart was necessary to create gold? Maybe the white stone would require a heart that didn't just belong to the fairest maiden, but the fairest *royal* maiden. A princess's heart. My heart.

The queen sent maidservants to attend to me and make me beautiful once more. Now I knew why—to make my appearance beautiful to ensure that my heart would be acceptable to the white stone for creating gold.

In fact, with the realization of her plans, many of my questions found answers. Now I understood why just after my eighteenth birthday, she'd plotted my murder separately from the Choosing Ball. In her greed, she hoped to have a heart for both gold and jewels. Perhaps she also thought that if my heart failed to produce the gold she sought, then she wouldn't have to compromise her production of jewels.

Now I understood why she'd never release Ruby to me or to Mikkel, because one day when Ruby came of age, she'd use Ruby's heart for the same purpose. Perhaps that's why the queen had worked so diligently all these years to find my cousin, because she wanted Queen Aurora's heart for her alchemy.

When the guards finally came for me, I told myself I was ready. If my outcast friends could somehow free Ruby and Mikkel, then I'd be able to bear going to my death, knowing that the two people I cared most about were safely in Scania.

As I walked through the long passageways, the heavy steps of the soldiers before and behind me tapped out an ominous rhythm, reminding me not only of how outnumbered my friends would be, but how unsafe against so many well-trained knights.

We exited through a side tower door and rounded the keep into the spacious inner bailey. I forced myself not to glance around and look for my friends. I didn't want to give away their presence or their positions. Nevertheless, my pulse thudded with expectation.

The thick castle walls rose on the southern side of the bailey and overlooked the sprawling capital city. To the north, mountainous cliffs formed an impenetrable wall. Imposing stone towers spiraled into the air, and I suspected the queen had relegated Mikkel to an isolated room at the top of one of those towers. I prayed Gregor had figured out a way to release him, though I didn't know how he would accomplish it.

The light-blue skies were the same shade as Mikkel's eyes, and my heart panged with longing for him. I hadn't been able to stop thinking about and reliving his declaration of love and his kisses from the feast.

I realized now that the queen had planned the feast and made me as beautiful as possible to beguile Mikkel. His ardor had proven the power of my beauty to sway him. And now she had strengthened her case of treason against me, demonstrating that I was in league with Mikkel and condemning him in the process.

While I'd anticipated she might hold Mikkel as ransom for Vilmar, I hadn't expected her threat to kill him. Surely she would relent and only hold him until Vilmar gave himself up? She wouldn't behead him and risk Scania's wrath at taking the life of one of their princes, would she?

At my appearance on the grassy knoll, the gathering of mostly noblemen grew silent. They stood on either side of the queen at the center of the bailey. A dozen paces from them was a sight that turned my stomach—a large smooth stone and the executioner, a man holding a double-bladed axe and wearing a black hood that covered his face except for the eye holes.

Farther away, servants stared from the windows and doorways of the thatched huts built against the inner wall. The buildings formed the soldiers' garrison, stables, smithy, apothecary, and other trades that made the castle self-sufficient.

Along the battlements, soldiers paused in their duties to peer down. I didn't need to count to know that four stood along the inner rim and four along the outer, in addition to the two in the gatehouse towers. With the half dozen who escorted me, along with others off duty in the nearby garrison, I didn't hold out much hope of an escape for myself. Nevertheless, I prayed for it for Mikkel and Ruby.

A quick look around told me Ruby wasn't present in the bailey, and my pulse stumbled, as did my faltering steps. Had I been amiss in my assumption the queen would make her watch me die? Perhaps the queen still had a shred of compassion left for her youngest child. More likely, she was ensuring that Ruby remained safeguarded for her future alchemy needs.

If only we'd been born boys like Ethelbard. As the heir to the throne, he rarely stayed in the same palace as the queen, and he was currently residing in one of the royal country estates near the eastern coast. Though he'd visited Kensington from time to time while growing up, I'd never gotten to know my brother well. From the little I'd learned, he was unlike my mother in just about every way. Perhaps she'd been able to tolerate him because she didn't feel threatened by him the same way she did with me.

What would he say once he discovered the queen had executed me? I doubted he would oppose her decision. He did everything the queen asked of him without question, just as our father had done.

Mikkel had accused me of following Irontooth without question. Had I done so not only with Irontooth but also with the queen? Perhaps I'd lived for so long trying to please my mother and gain her affection that I'd closed my eyes to her evil ways, hadn't allowed myself to see what she was truly capable of doing until it was too late.

The guards ushered me in front of the queen, who stood regally, as beautiful as always. Attired in a gown of fine gold, she shimmered in the sunshine. I understood now why she didn't accept Mikkel's offer of an alliance—she would soon have gold and no longer need any other country's aid. She would be powerful and wealthy enough on her own.

Lifting my chin, I stood unmoving before her. She waited, expecting me to kneel before her as I normally did. However, this time I wouldn't allow myself to care whether I pleased her or not. I held myself rigid and forced myself not to cower under her sharp gaze.

She nodded toward the castle garden at the rear of the keep. "Your beloved is arriving to watch."

I drew in a sharp breath at the sight of two soldiers leading Mikkel, gagged and bound, onto the green. They shoved him to a post, swiftly looped his arms overhead to a hook, and then sliced open his shirt, rendering his back bare. One of the soldiers held a scourge covered in bits of bone and rock. I shuddered, praying Gregor and the outcasts would strike before Mikkel had to suffer.

Just as soon as I lifted the prayer heavenward, the queen nodded at the soldier with the whip. He braced his feet, lifted the leather strip, and brought it down against Mikkel, the whistle and ensuing slap echoing in the air.

I screamed at the same instant Mikkel arched in agony as the jagged edges of the whip tore into his flesh. "No!" I started toward him but only managed two steps before a knight restrained me.

"Release him!" Frantic, I twisted to face the queen again. This time I dropped to my knees, forcing the knight to release his grip on me. I bowed low, pressing my face into the overlong grass. "Please, Your Majesty. I beg of you. He is of no consequence to you. 'Tis me you need, not him."

I didn't care that I was groveling. My good intention of standing up to her fled as my need to protect Mikkel swelled.

"I had considered keeping the prince locked away the same as Ruby," the queen said. "But I see he will be of use in ensuring your fullest cooperation."

Not only was she torturing Mikkel to bend me to her wishes, but Ruby was still stuck in the queen's grasp. All my efforts to free her had been for naught.

I kept my head bowed so the queen couldn't see how much I despised her. The hatred that had been building for months boiled near the surface, and I fisted my hands with the need to jump up, surround the queen's neck, and squeeze.

"Bitterness leads to bondage, but forgiveness sets us free." Sister Clare's wise words to Ruby echoed in my mind. I didn't want to forgive my mother, but I couldn't go to my death full of bitterness and hatred. I wanted to be free and at peace.

With my hair loose and shielding my face like a veil, I closed my eyes. *God, aid me in forgiving the queen for not loving me the way a mother should. Aid me in forgiving her, not for her sake but for mine. I want to be free.*

"'Tis a shame." The queen's tone was condescending. "To think that if you had remained content instead of aspiring to the throne, you might have become Prince Mikkel's wife."

"I did not aspire to the throne. We both know that. And I am already his wife." The words came out before I could stop them. What did it matter if the queen knew of our marriage? Matters couldn't get any worse.

The queen drew in a sharp breath. "What did you say?"

"I am married to Prince Mikkel."

She grabbed a fistful of my hair and yanked my head back, forcing me to look up at her. Strain creased her forehead and formed lines at the sides of her mouth, marring her beauty and showing her age. "You are lying."

I winced at the tight grip against my scalp. "No, Your Majesty. We are man and wife and have been since a fortnight after Midsummer's Eve."

Her eyes widened, revealing a panic I didn't understand. She stared at me as though she might slap me, then forced her features to relax. "'Tis of no consequence. Marriage is outlawed in Warwick until the age of twenty, thus your union is rendered void. I shall have the priests draw up annulment papers forthwith."

What difference did it make to her whether I was married? Unless . . .

My pulse skipped forward at double the speed. In addition to the other qualifications for the alchemy, she needed the heart of an *unmarried* woman. That was why she'd made the regulation for the marriage age in Warwick. And that was why now she wouldn't be able to use my heart for her alchemy process.

"Mikkel and I were not married in Warwick." I chose my words with care. Everything depended upon the next few moments. "We were wed in Norland on the Isle of Outcasts by a priest in front of both God and man as our witnesses."

"How dare you? You had no right to marry without my permission. All the more reason to execute you."

Though her tone and grip remained unyielding, something flickered in her eyes. Was it indecision? It couldn't be.

From the corner of my eye, I could see the confusion on her advisors' faces. They clearly had no notion of the queen's evil alchemy process and her use of a maiden's heart. I could expose her secret right now, but I sensed she would deny it and proceed to torture Mikkel until he died before my eyes.

But if I kept her secret and aided her efforts, I might be able to bargain for both Mikkel's and Ruby's lives. I had to try it now, before Gregor and my friends began their rescue attempt.

"I am of no use to you dead. But I would be of great value to you alive. I have the ability to find what you seek."

Her lips curved into a sneer. "And what do I seek?"

"Queen Aurora. I shall bring you her heart."

Her gaze locked with mine. She wanted to know if I understood the secrets of her alchemy.

I nodded.

"Kill her." She shoved me toward the stone.

"No!" The knights bent to pull me away from the queen, but I struggled to resist. "You have sought Queen Aurora her whole life and her keys to an ancient treasure. I shall find her and the keys so you can have the kingdom and the treasure that is rightfully yours."

Not only would she get Aurora's heart, but she would be able to restore her father's kingdom into a united Bryttania and also have a mythical treasure at her disposal.

The widening of the queen's eyes told me she'd

added up all the benefits and could see everything she had to gain. Without it she would have nothing.

As the guards began to drag me away, she held up a hand and stopped them. "How will you find her when no one else has succeeded?"

I looked pointedly at the men standing nearby and the need to speak more privately regarding the plans.

"Bring the prisoner to me," the queen commanded.

The soldiers pushed me back before her. They didn't relinquish me, and I knew this was as private an audience as I would have. "Aurora is my cousin, and she will trust me, especially if she believes I am running from you and trying to save my life."

The queen didn't respond except to study my face.

"If you free Mikkel and Ruby and allow them to come with me, then Aurora will believe we are refugees hiding from you, just as she is."

"You will win her trust and then betray her?" The queen released a mocking laugh. She knew me too well. Such betrayal wouldn't come naturally to me—would in fact go against everything I stood for.

And yet, how could I toss away this opportunity to save Mikkel and Ruby? It was my only chance at freedom. Surely once we were away from the castle and Kensington, we could escape from the country without needing to chase after Aurora.

"You are too weak to betray her."

"I shall do whatever I must in order to keep the ones I love safe." I glanced toward Mikkel where he hung, his back bleeding from his wounds.

"Then I shall keep Mikkel and Ruby until you return with Aurora."

"No." The word came out a weak plea, and the

moment it did, I realized I had to remain strong to fight this strong woman. "No." This time I spoke with confidence and force. "Even now, my friends are waiting to attack. You shall tell your soldiers to hold back, to give just enough effort to the fight and chase so it appears real. Then when we reach Aurora, she will take pity on my husband and me for having to flee from you. If she suspects otherwise, she will never allow me to get near her."

The clucking and squawking of the chickens on the bailey green filled the silence. After a moment, the queen shook her head and waved her hand in dismissal.

"She will be twenty this autumn, will she not?" I hastened to solidify the argument. "You have a little over two months in which to capture her before she will no longer be of use to you."

She narrowed her eyes upon me. And again, I held her gaze, making sure she knew I was well aware of why she needed Aurora.

"I have searched the Great Isle from top to bottom for Aurora. What makes you think you can succeed where my best soldiers have failed?"

"I believe she is somewhere in Inglewood Forest—"

"My men have searched there many times to no avail."

"On one occasion when Father and I hunted in the forest, we heard a rumor that Aurora had been spotted at Huntwell Fortress. I shall return there with the pretense of seeking their aid. And in so doing, I shall play upon their sympathies and discover the truth."

The queen regarded me again, and I prayed she was seriously considering my bargain.

I lifted my chin. "Two months. Now that you no longer have me, you cannot afford to waste another day."

She hesitated a moment longer. "Very well. I shall give you Mikkel. But I will not release Ruby until you bring Aurora directly to me."

My heart stuttered in protest, but her refusal wasn't unexpected. "Then we shall meet in the Boarshead Hunting Grounds by All Saints' Day. There we shall make an even exchange." The royal hunting lodge was located in northern Warwick within the section of Inglewood Forest I'd hunted in often with my father. Though it had been several years since I'd gone, I still knew the area well.

The queen didn't reply. Even if she gave me her word, she'd proven she wasn't trustworthy. I had the feeling she'd find an excuse for keeping Ruby no matter what I did. And no doubt, now that I'd alerted the queen to my suspicion of Aurora being in Inglewood Forest, she'd send more guards there to find Aurora before we did.

Even if she increased her efforts, she couldn't afford to spurn my offer, just in case I could locate Aurora where all others had failed. At least, that's what I was counting on.

"Have your soldiers position me at the stone table." I guessed once that happened, Gregor and the outcasts would finally strike. "When the onslaught begins, have everyone take cover so that no one dies today."

Before I could move away, she gripped my arm, digging her fingers in to my flesh. "You might be of use to me as a daughter after all. Do not let me down."

I wanted to tell her I wasn't doing this for her. That

I was no longer her daughter. And that I didn't care if I let her down. But I bit back the bitterness. It would do no good to spew it. Instead, I looked her full in the face and forced the words I knew I must say. "You have never loved me and likely never will. But I forgive you nevertheless."

With that, I turned away, allowing the guards to lead me toward the stone table and praying that when my friends attacked, she wouldn't change her mind and kill me after all.

Chapter 24

MY BACK BURNED AS THOUGH IT HAD BEEN SET ON FIRE. However, the pain in my heart was worse than in my body. I couldn't bear seeing Pearl and knowing that within moments she'd lay her head down on the stone and the executioner would end her life.

As I'd languished in the barren tower room, I'd done little else but plot and pray. Unfortunately, I hadn't been able to find a way out of the trap the queen had laid for us.

When the guards had brought me down to the castle green and stripped me of my shirt, I guessed then that the queen intended to use me to subdue Pearl. I wanted to implore Pearl to remain strong and not give in to any demands, but the queen had apparently anticipated that and gagged me.

Now as I hung from the whipping post, misery mingled with the pain and I bent my head. If I happened to survive, I didn't want to become the next king of Scania. I didn't deserve it, not after I'd failed to save the woman I loved.

Vilmar was the better man after all.

No, I had to stop comparing myself to Vilmar. Hadn't I learned that already in my Testing? To stop judging others, even myself? I might not be able to easily win people over the way Vilmar could. But perhaps a king was stronger if he didn't worry about pleasing people and instead lived by a higher code of honor.

As the guards led Pearl toward the executioner's stone, she struggled against them. I expected the queen to motion toward me and demand additional lashing for Pearl's lack of cooperation. But she didn't bother to glance my direction, almost as if she'd forgotten I was there.

I twisted my hands, working to loosen the binding. From the moment the guard had looped my hands to the hook, I'd realized his knot wasn't secure. He'd probably assumed I'd be in too much pain to attempt to free myself. And though just the one lash had torn the flesh from my back, I forced myself to concentrate on the knot.

Fortunately, the guard was distracted by Pearl's angst, and I worked faster, slipping my hands up and jostling the binding, loosening it even more. When the guard glanced at me, I ceased, then resumed my efforts as his attention shifted away.

The knights shoved Pearl to her knees and forced her to lower her head. Desperate now, I tugged one hand free, my pulse spurting forward with the need to do something. My sights narrowed upon the belt of my guard, the sword and knife sheathed within reach along with his whip. Could I divest him of at least one or maybe two of the weapons?

I jerked my other hand loose, jumped to my feet, and grabbed his knife before he realized I was no longer bound. I threw the knife at the executioner and then lunged for the guard's sword. He was swifter than me and lashed out with the whip, forcing me to dive out of reach.

Shouts rose up within the bailey. My time was running out. I had to act now if I had any hope of saving Pearl. I rushed at another nearby guard, tackling him and unsheathing his knife in the same moment. Though he wrestled with me, my distress gave me an advantage. I sliced him, wounding him and pushing him to the ground.

A clamor erupted around me—arrows raining down from the inner walls and the guards moving to surround and protect the queen. I didn't waste time trying to figure out what was happening. Instead, I grabbed up a sword discarded on the ground and bolted toward the executioner's block and Pearl. She was already on her feet and stumbling away, her countenance distraught, until she located me.

"Mikkel!" She veered in my direction. "We need to go! Now!"

I sprinted toward her, intending to pick her up and carry her out of the castle if need be. But she secured my hand and began to run toward the gatehouse, dragging me in her wake. I didn't know what was going on, but I suspected Gregor had helped orchestrate a rescue effort of some kind. Who had he rallied to join him?

As we passed through the inner gate into the outer bailey, I picked up my pace and took the lead, forcing Pearl to keep up. The gatehouse loomed ahead, and I was relieved to see that the gates were still open. The guards would close them at any moment to trap us inside. And yet, as we dodged chickens and dogs along with tradesmen and their carts, no one tried to stop us.

When we ran into the shadowed interior of the

gateway, a hooded man jumped from one of the guard tower ladders and dropped into our path. I raised my sword to thrust him away. But as he turned to reveal silver hair and iron-studded teeth, I halted the momentum of the sword.

Irontooth was here? "How—?"

"We must be on our way." Pearl started up again. "There will be time for questions later."

Irontooth's knife was unsheathed and coated in blood, informing me why the gatehouse guards hadn't yet tried to impede our exit. He may have stopped the two in charge of the gatehouse, but the other queen's men would be on our trail erelong. Pearl was right. We had to make haste.

I glanced back toward the outer bailey and the inner green still in chaos. Were Gregor and the other outcasts positioned inside wreaking havoc? If so, how had they managed to get so close? And what would happen once the battle was over? Did they have an escape plan, or would they be trapped and suffer on our account? "The others? We can't leave them."

"They'll soon be on their way"—Irontooth shoved me through the gatehouse—"and lose themselves in the crowds."

"We shall be fine." Pearl spoke with more assurance than the situation warranted.

Though I didn't know how we would manage to outmaneuver our enemy, we started forward at a run. I took the lead and Irontooth the rear, and once again we dodged people and animals alike. I expected shouts to trail us and arrows to slice the air, but as we careened down the winding path, weaving through the other travelers, no one stopped us.

When we reached the bottom, Irontooth led us to a nearby alley that was deserted except for a mule cart loaded with hay. He headed directly for the cart and jumped onto it with a nod at the back. "Climb on and hide in the hay."

I plunged into the hay first, then pulled Pearl in. The cart was narrow, and Pearl had to sit in front of me. She spread the hay over the top of us with Irontooth piling on even more until it covered us completely.

As the cart moved forward, the bumping and rocking was so jarring, I was afraid the hay would fall away and expose us. But it remained thick and heavy above us, sweltering and itchy, especially against my bloody back.

Pearl jostled against me, her breathing still heavy. The escape from the inner bailey had been too easy. And so had the run from the castle. Something wasn't right. Though I had a thousand questions, we had to speak sparingly. We were still in too much peril of being discovered and needed to use extra caution until we were well away from the city limits.

I slid my arms around Pearl's waist and tugged her against me. For a moment, she kept herself rigid.

"Your back is hurt," she whispered.

"It will be fine." Though fire still burned over my flesh from my wounds, I ignored the pain and instead focused on the woman in my arms. I pressed my face into her hair and breathed her in.

She crossed her arms over mine and squeezed me as though she never planned to let go. I hoped she wouldn't.

Chapter 25

Pearl

We traveled for over an hour without stopping. As uncomfortable and hot as the hay was, I relished resting in Mikkel's arms, knowing how close I'd come to losing him forever. The bumpiness of the route and the noise from the wheels made whispering imposs-ible. And even though we both had a great deal to say to one another, we rested quietly.

Finally, the cart rolled to a stop. A moment later, it bobbed as Irontooth descended. The rise and fall of Mikkel's chest stopped. His body tensed around mine. And he held himself motionless.

Though some of the hay had fallen away, we were still hidden. No one would know we were underneath, not unless they'd followed us from the castle.

"You can come out," Irontooth said. "We're safe for now."

I sat up and broke through the hay, shoving and kicking it away. Before I could crawl off the cart, Mikkel caught me and pulled me back. This time I landed on his lap, and before I could say anything, he cupped my cheeks and pressed his lips to mine, kissing me greedily, as though he'd been waiting for the past hour to do this very thing and couldn't go another second.

I responded, letting my relief well up into the kiss. I wrapped my arms around his neck, right where I wanted to be in a place I never wanted to leave.

"You can kiss later," Irontooth said, his tone gruff but laced with humor. "This is as far as we can go in the cart. We have to keep moving in order to stay ahead of the queen's soldiers. And we need to make it to the rendezvous spot, where we'll meet up with Gregor and the others."

I broke away from Mikkel. For a moment, we rested with our foreheads touching and breaths mingling.

Mikkel was the first to lean away. As he did, I became aware of our surroundings, the foothills rising in front of us, the boulders surrounded by yew and juniper, the dark forest of evergreens farther up the slopes.

I recognized the area north of Kensington beyond Wraith Lake. The terrain was rocky and rough but consisted of many hiding places. Clearly, Irontooth was familiar enough with Warwick to know where to go, or he'd gleaned the information while plotting the escape.

"We're traveling by foot the rest of the distance," Irontooth continued, "so we can move faster."

I climbed down from the cart and brushed the hay from my gown. Mikkel crawled off and took the cloak Irontooth held out to him. He started to wrap it around his bare torso, but I grabbed it and forced it away. "I shall clean and doctor your wounds first."

"We'll have time for that later." He started to drape the cloak again.

I wrenched it from his hold. "I shall do it now."

"And risk capture again?"

"We have no need for haste."

"Why not?"

"The queen's soldiers will not follow us."

"And how can that be when the queen has condemned you to death?" He crossed his arms over his bare chest, drawing my attention to his rounded muscles.

A flush moved into my cheeks, and I hastily returned the cloak. I waited for him to cover himself before continuing. "The queen no longer has need of my heart and has better use for me alive than dead."

Mikkel's light-blue eyes were intense, filled with all the fervor and determination I loved. "And why did the queen need your heart in the first place?"

I explained all I'd learned since arriving: how Mikkel had been right about Grendel, how the queen kept the monster for her own purposes, how she'd used the hearts of maidens in her alchemy to create jewels, and how she believed the heart of a royal maiden was the secret ingredient in alchemy for making gold.

As I spoke, the furrows in Mikkel's forehead deepened. "If your heart can aid her alchemy, why does she no longer have need for it?"

"Because the heart must belong to an unmarried young woman."

"Then our marriage saved you?"

I nodded.

Perched on a boulder, Irontooth guffawed. "Does this mean you'll be rewarding me for forcing you into the marriage?"

Mikkel managed a grin. "I shall declare you a national hero for your deed." Even as he teased Irontooth, his expression remained guarded as though he sensed there was more to my explanation.

I shifted, tangling in my ruby gown and wishing I could free myself from the heavy garment every bit as much as I could free myself from the bargain I'd struck with the queen. The more I considered my deal, the more ashamed I was of what I'd done. I didn't want to tell Mikkel, but I'd already deceived him with my veil and had to move forward with truth henceforth.

"I told the queen I would bring her another royal heart." I confessed my deed before I lost the courage. "A heart belonging to Queen Aurora of Mercia. Since my mother has been attempting to find and kill my cousin since birth, I told her I would help her find Aurora."

Mikkel didn't react and instead waited as I explained everything I'd spoken to the queen about— the two months remaining to find Aurora as well as my suspicion that she was in Inglewood Forest.

"'Twas the only way to save you," I finished. "And 'twill be the only way the queen agrees to release Ruby to me.

"But . . ."

"But I cannot betray Aurora and deliver her to the queen. However, if I do not, she will never give me Ruby." I held up my hands, the helplessness of my situation settling upon me. "Tell me what I must do, Mikkel."

He stared off into the distance for a moment, his brow pinching. "We must find Aurora right away, not only to protect her, but to gain her cooperation in the fight against the queen."

"We?" I shook my head. "No, I shall do this alone. You must go back to the Isle of Outcasts and finish your Testing." I couldn't allow him to give up becoming king for me.

Irontooth shook his head. "He'll never be accepted back now that the truth is out about who you both are. I won't either and neither will the others who came with me." Irontooth explained how someone had found one of the notices the queen had posted offering the reward for Pearl. It hadn't taken long to connect the notice to Pearl's reason for traveling to Warwick and to understand who she really was. Irontooth, Felicity, Toad, Humphrey, and a few others had remained loyal. But as a result, the rest of the outcasts had joined together and forced them to leave.

"I regret causing so much trouble for you," I said once he'd finished his tale.

"It worked out for the best." Irontooth stood and stretched. "After how you sacrificed yourselves to help me save Felicity, I knew I needed to come to your aid."

We talked for a few more minutes about Irontooth's plans for the future, and he insisted he would stay with us wherever we might go until we were able to rescue Ruby. Then, as though sensing my need for a moment of privacy with Mikkel, he wandered over to the mule and began to unhitch the cart.

I nodded my thanks before facing Mikkel. "You must find a way to finish your Testing."

He grasped my hands as though he never meant to let go. "I've learned that I can do my Testing anywhere, that it's not the place that matters but doing the hard things that help us grow."

"But you are meant to be a king—"

He brought a finger to my lips and silenced me. "If God wills it, he will bring it about in his time and in his way. And if he doesn't, I shall accept my fate. In the meantime, I shall fight beside you as we seek to do what is true and right."

I paused to take in his declaration, still uncertain whether I should allow him to abandon the Testing. He'd shown himself to be a man of honor and principle who would sacrifice much for others. How could I deny him that? "What if we cannot find Aurora?"

"We shall enlist Kresten's aid. He has lived in Inglewood Forest for his Testing these many months and will be able to help."

"And what if Aurora has no desire to join our fight against the queen?"

"Surely she will once we tell her how Queen Margery has discovered the secrets of alchemy. If Queen Margery's alchemy is left unchecked, she could become one of the most powerful queens in the world. As such, she would pose an even greater threat to Mercia and many other countries, including Scania."

Everything Mikkel said was as wise as always. The battle against the queen wasn't simply about freeing Ruby. It was much more serious than that. "She must be stopped."

"And Aurora is the one to help us do it."

"Then you are not angry with me for bargaining on my cousin's life?"

"Of course not." He reached for my hands again and drew me nearer. "You thought quickly and used the queen's greed to your advantage."

"She will not hold to her end of the agreement. She has never been trustworthy."

The hard set of his jaw told me he'd learned that lesson all too well the day of the feast when she'd locked us both away. "She may be a hypocrite and full of lies. But we do not have to follow that path, and I pray we can have honesty between us henceforth."

I nodded. He was referring to my veil. "I am heartily sorry for any untruths in the past and vow I shall be honest from this day forward."

"And do you vow never to rush off without me again? That whatever peril or challenges the future may bring, we will face adversity together, side by side?"

"I vow it."

Though he winced at the brush of his cloak against the wounds on his back, he held himself with the bearing of royalty, his back straight, his chin lifted, his lips firm with determination, reminding me of how he'd looked that day he'd run the gauntlet on the island. He was a strong man, one who only made me stronger in return.

I pressed my hand to his scruffy cheek. Over-whelming love for him swelled inside. "I didn't mean what I said at the feast. I do love you."

His lips curved into a smile, and he pulled me into his arms. "I know you do."

"You do?"

"You have loved me since the first day we met."

I swatted him but couldn't contain a smile of my

own. "You think too highly of yourself."

"I am right, am I not?"

"No—"

"I admit to starting to fall in love with you the first day we met."

After the months of wearing the veil, I'd felt strangely bare the past few days and was self-conscious as his attention lingered on my face. "And I admit I am relieved to know you care more for who I am than what I look like."

"I have learned that what lies beneath the surface is much more important than appearances." He brushed a finger down my cheek to my jaw, sending tingles over my skin. "But I cannot deny I am just as beguiled by your outer beauty as I am with who you are on the inside."

I leaned in to his touch. "Shall I go back to wearing a veil so I do not beguile you, my lord?"

"Don't even think about it. For then I shall not be able to do this." He angled in and captured my lips in a kiss, one that took away every coherent thought.

"Aw, come on now." Irontooth's call broke through our kiss. "I said you can kiss later."

"It is later," Mikkel murmured through another kiss. "It will always be one moment later."

I leaned away from him, my smile widening. "Does that mean you will always be kissing me?"

"Yes, always and forever." As he pressed his lips to mine again, I lifted up on my toes to kiss him back, showing him I would accept those kisses and love him always and forever too.

Chapter 26

Queen Margery

I caressed the golden box, tracing the intricate ancient engravings that covered it. The white stone inside was shaped and sized like a young maiden's heart. The candelabra on the chapel altar made the stone glow, revealing all of its beauty. Though as clear as a diamond, it contained hues of precious gems and was woven with intricate threads of gold.

Little had I known during my early years of searching to uncover its mysteries that many clues were deep in the stone itself, clues I'd discovered through too many failed experiments and trials.

As much as the beautiful stone beckoned to me, I didn't dare touch it. I'd witnessed the power it had over the servants we'd used in our experiments. In every single instance without fail, anyone who came into contact with the stone itself always fell into a deep sleep of unconsciousness and eventually died.

The stone had a life and will of its own. Though many kings and queens before me had claimed it was cursed, they'd comprehended that the cost for its destruction was too high.

I'd learned the cost for its fulfillment was also high. But over the years, I'd determined to pay the price so that I might earn the distinction of being the first to make gold.

For so long, I'd hoped to avoid using Pearl's heart when she came of age, had increased my efforts to find my niece instead. But with every passing year of failing to locate Aurora, I'd closed myself off to Pearl and hardened my heart toward her. Eventually, I'd accepted the fact that I would have to sacrifice Pearl if I had any chance of accomplishing what no one else had ever been able to do.

I wanted to think I would have been able to go through with the beheading, that I wouldn't have given way to the pressure building inside my chest to call off the execution. But when she'd delivered the news of her marriage to Mikkel, a strange tension had eased from my body. Had I been relieved? Was there still a part of me that I hadn't been able to harden toward my flesh and blood?

Was that why I'd so readily agreed to her plan and set her free? And why I hadn't gone through with beheading her as I should have? After all, she'd made clear enough that she understood the secrets of my alchemy—had likely learned them from Ruby. That alone was enough to silence her.

Instead of the beheading today, I should have sent her away to be murdered as I'd done for last year's hunting expedition when a part of me had known I wouldn't be able to watch her die, not even in the yearly sacrifice to Grendel.

With a sigh of frustration, I traced the rim of the golden box and gazed upon the white stone, trying to absorb its power and life. Today I'd shown a moment of weakness, and I couldn't let it happen again. After all, the ancient parchment in the secret compartment of the box stated that only the hardest of hearts could ever do what was required to make use of the white stone.

"Are you ready, Your Majesty?" My priest bowed his tonsured head and waved a hand toward the velvet-lined chest that was cushioned inside another chest.

I ran my fingers along the engravings of the golden box one last time, and then carefully lowered the lid, securing the white stone inside. "Yes, I am ready."

I took a step back and allowed the priest and his companion to lift the golden box from its sacred pedestal and lower it into the awaiting chest. A special cart was ready for the golden box, one I used for transporting the white stone during the yearly trip to the Gemstone Mountains and the mine pits.

This year, however, we wouldn't be journeying up into the mountains. Instead, we would go north to Inglewood Forest and Boarshead Hunting Lodge.

And I was ready. I'd failed with Pearl. But I wouldn't with Aurora.

Already, my elite knights were following Pearl and Mikkel. They would make use of every clue Pearl unearthed in hunting for Aurora. And they would find the young queen first. They must. I knew Pearl was too soft and sentimental to carry through in delivering Aurora over to me.

"Ruby is ready to go, Your Majesty," said one of the

guards from the chapel's doorway.

"Very well. You must deliver her to Boarshead Hunting Lodge without any incidents."

The guard bowed, his armor clinking in readiness for his mission. Though I'd wanted to leave Ruby behind and far away from Pearl, I suspected I would have need of the girl in one form or another.

Prince Mikkel would likely seek out the aid of his brother Prince Vilmar and perhaps even the help of his youngest brother, Prince Kresten—though I had yet to learn where he was conducting his Testing. If I could lure the Scanian princes to Boarshead Hunting Lodge, then I would have a greater chance of eliminating them, especially now that Mikkel and Vilmar knew the secrets of my alchemy.

I was familiar enough with the rules of the Testing to know that King Christian couldn't break with tradition to come to the aid of his sons by sending his forces to Warwick to rescue them. While I might incur King Christian's wrath for killing his sons, I wasn't concerned. Making an enemy of him wouldn't matter once I had the power to make gold. I wouldn't need Scania or any other nation's friendship. Instead, they would grovel before me.

The priest finished securing the golden box and then motioned toward the two chapel guards to come carry the chest.

As they lifted the container with utmost care, I preceded them, the white stone never far from my presence. "Let us be on our way."

I would find Aurora and the Scanian princes, and I vowed to destroy them once and for all.

Jody Hedlund is the best-selling author of over forty books and is the winner of numerous awards. She writes sweet historical romances with plenty of sizzle. Find out more at jodyhedlund.com.

More Sweet Medieval Romance from Jody Hedlund

The Fairest Maidens

Beholden

Upon the death of her wealthy father, Lady Gabriella is condemned to work in Warwick's gem mine. As she struggles to survive the dangerous conditions, her kindness and beauty shine as brightly as the jewels the slaves excavate. While laboring, Gabriella plots how to avenge her father's death and stop Queen Margery's cruelty.

Beguiled

Princess Pearl flees for her life after her mother, Queen Margery, tries to have her killed during a hunting expedition. Pearl finds refuge on the Isle of Outcasts among criminals and misfits, disguising her face with a veil so no one recognizes her. She lives for the day when she can return to Warwick and rescue her sister, Ruby, from the queen's clutches.

Besotted

Queen Aurora of Mercia has spent her entire life deep in Inglewood Forest, hiding from Warwick's Queen Margery, who seeks her demise. As the time draws near for Aurora to take the throne, she happens upon a handsome woodcutter. Although friendship with outsiders is forbidden and dangerous, she cannot stay away from the charming stranger.

The Lost Princesses

Always: Prequel Novella

On the verge of dying after giving birth to twins, the queen of Mercia pleads with Lady Felicia to save her infant daughters. With the castle overrun by King Ethelwulf's invading army, Lady Felicia vows to do whatever she can to take the newborn princesses and their three-year-old sister to safety, even though it means sacrificing everything she holds dear, possibly her own life.

Evermore

Raised by a noble family, Lady Adelaide has always known she's an orphan. Little does she realize she's one of the lost princesses and the true heir to Mercia's throne . . . until a visitor arrives at her family estate, reveals her birthright as queen, and thrusts her into a quest for the throne whether she's ready or not.

Foremost

Raised in an isolated abbey, Lady Maribel desires nothing more than to become a nun and continue practicing her healing arts. She's carefree and happy with her life . . . until a visitor comes to the abbey and reveals her true identity as one of the lost princesses.

Hereafter

Forced into marriage, Emmeline has one goal—to escape. But Ethelrex takes his marriage vows seriously, including his promise to love and cherish his wife, and he has no intention of letting Emmeline get away. As the battle for the throne rages, will the prince be able to win the battle for Emmeline's heart?

Knights of Brethren

Enamored

Having been raised by her childless aunt and uncle, the king and queen, Princess Elinor finds herself the only heir to the throne of Norvegia. As she comes of age, she must choose a husband to rule beside her, but she struggles to make her selection from among a dozen noblemen during a weeklong courtship.

Entwined

After growing up on a remote farm, Lis learns she is the rightful heir to the throne of Norvegia. Even as she does her part to thwart a dangerous plot against the king, she resists pursuing her new identity and resigns herself to a simple life helping her elderly father with their farm.

Ensnared

Nursemaid to the Earl of Likness's two young daughters, Mikaela despises the earl for his cruelty to his subjects, and she longs for the day when she can make a difference in the lives of her suffering friends and family.

Enriched

Lady Karina lives in a convent and expects to become a nun someday. When her wealthy father asks her to help his textile business become more successful by marrying one of the popular Knights of Brethren, Karina complies, ever the dutiful daughter.

Enflamed

When Sylvi Prestegard discovers that her father has arranged for her to marry a wealthy nobleman known for his thieving ways, she's desperate to avoid the union. She turns to her childhood friend Espen, a Knight of Brethren, counting on his loyalty and kindness to help her escape.

Entrusted

Hoping to minimize the death and destruction of the coming war, Princess Birgitta of Swaine leads the Dark Warriors as part of her brother King Canute's efforts to take the throne of Norvegia. As she engages in a skirmish with a band of elite Knights of Brethren, she's kidnapped by Kristoffer Prestegard, a cunning warrior.

The Noble Knights

The Vow

Young Rosemarie finds herself drawn to Thomas, the son of the nearby baron. But just as her feelings begin to grow, a man carrying the Plague interrupts their hunting party. While in forced isolation, Rosemarie begins to contemplate her future—could it include Thomas? Could he be the perfect man to one day rule beside her and oversee her parents' lands?

An Uncertain Choice

Due to her parents' promise at her birth, Lady Rosemarie has been prepared to become a nun on the day she turns eighteen. Then, shortly before her birthday, a friend of her father's enters the kingdom and proclaims her parents' will left a second choice—if Rosemarie can marry before the eve of her eighteenth year, she will be exempt from the ancient vow.

A Daring Sacrifice

In a reverse twist on the Robin Hood story, a young medieval maiden stands up for the rights of the mistreated, stealing from the rich to give to the poor. All the while, she fights against her cruel uncle who has taken over the land that is rightfully hers.

For Love & Honor

Lady Sabine is harboring a skin blemish, one that if revealed could cause her to be branded as a witch, put her life in danger, and damage her chances of making a good marriage. After all, what nobleman would want to marry a woman so flawed?

A Loyal Heart

When Lady Olivia's castle is besieged, she and her sister are taken captive and held for ransom by her father's enemy, Lord Pitt. Loyalty to family means everything to Olivia. She'll save her sister at any cost and do whatever her father asks—even if that means obeying his order to steal a sacred relic from her captor.

A Worthy Rebel

While fleeing an arranged betrothal to a heartless lord, Lady Isabelle becomes injured and lost. Rescued by a young peasant man, she hides her identity as a noblewoman for fear of reprisal from the peasants who are bitter and angry toward the nobility.

A complete list of my novels can be found at jodyhedlund.com.

Would you like to know when my next book is available? You can sign up for my newsletter, become my friend on Goodreads, like me on Facebook, or follow me on Twitter.

Newsletter: jodyhedlund.com
Goodreads:
goodreads.com/author/show/3358829.Jody_Hedlund
Facebook: facebook.com/AuthorJodyHedlund
Twitter: @JodyHedlund

The more reviews a book has, the more likely other readers are to find it. If you have a minute, please leave a rating or review. I appreciate all reviews, whether positive or negative.